Secrets
in the SNOW

Other Novels of Intrigue and Romance

The Revelation of Louisa May

Always Emily

Nobody's Secret

Prisoners in the Palace

Secrets

in the SNOW

A NOVEL OF INTRIGUE AND ROMANCE BY

MICHAELA MacCOLL

CHRONICLE BOOKS

SAN FRANCISCO

Library of Congress Cataloging-in-Publication Data:

Names: MacColl, Michaela, author.

Title: Secrets in the snow : a novel of intrigue and romance / by Michaela MacColl.

Description: San Francisco : Chronicle Books, [2016] | Summary: The young Jane Austen is not particularly interested in getting married, although she does find the mysterious Mr. Lefroy an intriguing possibility—but first she has to deal with the accusation that her cousin Eliza is a French spy, and solve a murder.

Identifiers: LCCN 2015047480 | ISBN 9781452133584 (alk. paper)

Subjects: LCSH: Austen, Jane, 1775-1817—Juvenile fiction. | Women authors, English—19th century—Juvenile fiction. | Detective and mystery stories. | Great Britain—History—1789-1820—Juvenile fiction. | France—History—Revolution, 1789-1799—Juvenile fiction. | CYAC: Mystery and detective stories. | Austen, Jane, 1775-1817—Fiction. | Authors, English—Fiction. | Great Britain—History—1789-1820—Fiction. | France—History—Revolution, 1789-1799—Fiction. | GSAFD: Mystery fiction. | Historical fiction.

Classification: LCC PZ7.M13384 Se 2016 | DDC 813.6—dc23 LC record available at http://lccn.loc.gov/2015047480ISBN 978-1-4521-3358-4

Manufactured in China.

Design by Lisa Schneller and Kayla Ferriera.
Typeset in Hoefler Text, Copperplate, and Shelley Allegro.

10 9 8 7 6 5 4 3 2 1

Chronicle Books LLC
680 Second Street
San Francisco, California 94107

Chronicle Books—we see things differently.
Become part of our community at www.chroniclebooks.com/teen.

To Max and Madi

CHAPTER 1

*"What have wealth or grandeur
to do with happiness?"
"Grandeur has but little," said Elinor,
"but wealth has much to do with it."*
SENSE AND SENSIBILITY

$\mathcal{J}$ane lay in bed, listening to the sounds only heard in a rich man's house. The slight creak as the door was shoved open by a servant's hip. The slight clink of china as the tray was deposited on the bedside table. The rattle of curtain rings as the heavy drapes were drawn back. The thud of coal being fed to the fire. All done without any effort on Jane's part.

The steamy aroma of freshly made tea—measured generously and never reused—crept like tendrils of fog through the room.

Slowly, Jane opened her eyes, blinking against the pale winter sunlight. She stretched her fingers and toes to all the corners of the narrow bed.

"Cassandra?" Jane whispered. "Are you awake?"

From across the spacious room, Jane heard a gentle yawn, then her sister answered. "Good morning, Jane. I smell tea."

"Don't you think tea smells better when you don't have to make it yourself?"

"I feel quite indolent," Cassandra admitted. "How will I ever go home again and have to do for myself?"

"Don't worry, dear Cass, our brother's wife will make sure you earn your keep."

"Jane! That's unkind," Cassandra scolded, but there was laughter in her voice. "Elizabeth needs our help to prepare for the next baby."

They had arrived at their brother Edward's palatial home by hired carriage the evening before. Jane and Cassandra's means were as modest as their elder brother's were exalted. When Edward was twelve, the Knight family, cousins to the Austens, had adopted him. Rich as Croesus, they lacked only an heir to their fortune. Edward was more than happy to change his name in exchange for a large estate.

"Elizabeth has a fortune and an army of servants," Jane reminded her. "She always takes pain to make it clear that we aren't welcome houseguests, but Edward's poor relations."

"Aren't we?" Cassandra asked simply.

"I'm in no mood to be clear-eyed this morning," Jane said, sweeping the blankets away and leaping out of bed. She pulled her soft wool shawl around her shoulders and went to the window to consider the weather. "The weather is fine enough for a walk before breakfast," she said, pouring herself a cup of the strong Indian tea and adding a generous spoonful of sugar. "Would you like some tea?"

"Not yet. How can you be so vigorous this early?" Cassandra said with a shake of her head. She pulled her blankets up to her nose. "I'm still exhausted from our journey."

"I've time for a long walk round Godmersham Park before breakfast," Jane said. The park was lovely in the summer and autumn, but now in the dead of winter it had a desolate air. She would have the paths to herself, which suited her admirably.

Jane quickly pulled her corset on over her chemise and slipped into a morning gown. She exchanged her slippers for walking boots and let herself out of the room, leaving Cassandra dozing.

When Jane returned from her usual vigorous walk, the hem of her skirt was wet and her boots were covered with mud. Rather than go in the front door so disheveled, she slipped through the tall doors that led from the garden to the library. She stopped short when she saw that her brother was sitting in front of one of the fireplaces.

"Jane!" He jumped up and embraced her. Edward was the very image of an English country squire, heavyset and blond with a florid complexion. "I'm sorry I wasn't here last night to greet you properly. I had a meeting with the regimental commander," he said, looking pleased with himself. "My goodness, it's already almost ten o'clock. We had better go to breakfast. Elizabeth hates if I'm late."

"I'll just change my clothes . . ."

"Nonsense. We want to see you, not your dress. How like a woman to think of changing one's clothes instead of eating the best meal of the day."

"I doubt that Elizabeth will be of the same opinion regarding my attire," Jane said waspishly.

"Don't be like that, Jane," Edward harrumphed. "Elizabeth means well." Jane smiled to see that away from his shrewish wife, her brother still resembled the sweet lad she remembered.

She followed Edward into the blue pastel drawing room where breakfast was waiting. Her sister-in-law was a handsome woman; her pale blond looks suited her drawing room. Jane noticed the fleeting frown as Elizabeth's glance took in Jane's unfashionable bonnet and filthy petticoat. She wondered how long it would take for Elizabeth to feel compelled to comment on her sister-in-law's appearance.

"Mr. Knight, Jane—there you are!" Elizabeth exclaimed. "I wondered where you two were."

Jane quickly glanced at Cassandra, who hid her smile behind her hand. Elizabeth must have been complaining about their tardiness. The only other guests, Colonel Waring and his wife, were drinking their tea and nibbling at toast.

"Colonel, Mrs. Waring," said Edward with a slight bow. "And Cassandra—so lovely to see you." Edward put his arm around Jane. "And look who I found sneaking into my library! Knowing how Jane likes to read, I'll have to count the books when she leaves." As Edward laughed heartily at his own joke, Jane tried to keep herself from wincing.

"Jane, have you been outside already?" Elizabeth asked, her eyebrows lifted. "It's so damp." She leaned slightly over the table to catch a glimpse of Jane's shoes. "And muddy."

"The weather is very fine," Jane replied, smiling to herself that Elizabeth couldn't even wait a full minute before criticizing her.

"So long as it doesn't snow, we'll have hunting through next week," the Colonel said. He looked like exactly what he was: a military man with a good income and a tendency to enjoy port a little too much.

"Good morning, Miss Austen," Mrs. Waring said. "Did you really go walking?"

"I'm used to keeping country hours, Mrs. Waring. At home in Steventon, we don't usually have a formal breakfast. We just toast bread by the fire."

"The deprivations of my youth!" Edward laughed heartily again.

Cassandra smiled politely while Jane bit her tongue. It was fine for Edward, with all his wealth, to joke, but in a few weeks his sisters would return to the same economizing.

Jane consoled herself with the sideboard filled with rich pastries. Her mouth watered when she saw the honey cake. Cassandra had a slice of plum cake and brioche on her plate, while Mrs. Waring had confined herself to toast but was indulging in hot chocolate.

"My goodness, Jane. You must restrain yourself or forfeit your figure," Elizabeth exclaimed.

"Jane can eat anything and never grow larger," Cassandra assured her sister-in-law.

Colonel Waring was reading the latest newspaper from London. Looking up, he addressed Edward. "I see the French are up to their usual tricks in the Mediterranean. Our navy will have to be quick to put a stop to it."

Jane and Cassandra exchanged concerned looks. Two of their older brothers were in the navy.

England and France had been at war for the past three years. So far the French had not dared set foot on English soil, but everyone knew the danger was real. Even here in the country, the rumors flew that French spies were everywhere.

Jane slathered fresh butter on her cake and asked, "If you are finished with the newspaper, Colonel Waring, perhaps I could have it?"

Elizabeth drew in a scandalized breath. Edward was grinning. Colonel and Mrs. Waring looked shocked. A hint of condescension in her voice, Mrs. Waring said, "Elizabeth, I had no idea your household was so permissive."

"It is not," Elizabeth said sharply. "Jane, I realize that you live a rusticated life in your little parsonage, but at the finer homes a young lady need never read the newspaper. It's a vulgar habit. Edward will tell you the news you need to hear."

Jane slowly put down the butter knife. "Firstly, dearest Elizabeth, I am quite capable of reading the newspaper myself. Secondly, our brothers are in the navy, so naturally Cassandra and I are deeply interested in any news from the Mediterranean." She paused, waiting for her sister to speak. "Aren't we, Cassandra?" Jane asked pointedly.

Cassandra's face was crimson. "We do worry so for Francis and Charles. This dreadful war is claiming so many of our finest young men."

Elizabeth flushed with embarrassment. "Of course, Jane. We are all concerned about the war. Mr. Knight and the Colonel are working closely with the regiment stationed at New Romney." Edward nodded solemnly.

"Since we are agreed that the news of the war is important, Colonel, may I again trouble you for the paper?" Jane inquired.

Grudgingly Colonel Waring handed the broadsheet to Jane.

Elizabeth pressed her lips tightly together. Her disapproval was interrupted by a footman carrying a letter on a silver tray. He murmured in Elizabeth's ear.

"A letter for you, Jane," Elizabeth said. "It arrived with the first post."

Jane broke the red wax seal and unfolded the thick paper. She scanned it and then smiled.

"Good news, I trust," Edward said.

"Indeed. It's from our cousin Eliza."

"Edward's cousin is the Comtesse De Feuillide," Elizabeth said to Mrs. Waring, who looked suitably impressed.

"*Our* cousin is staying with her friends in London and planning on coming to Steventon in a fortnight," Jane said. "But her hostess has fallen ill. She thought to come to the parsonage, but . . ." She let her voice trail off, inviting Elizabeth's response.

"You must have her come here!" Elizabeth said eagerly. Jane nodded, knowing that hosting a countess, even one whose title came from France, would be a social coup for her sister-in-law.

"Are you sure you have enough staff to accommodate her?" Jane asked innocently. "Ow!" She glared at Cassandra, whose pointed shoe had found her shin.

"Stop it, Jane," Edward said. "Naturally Eliza should come here. She's family."

"De Feuillide? It sounds French," Colonel Waring said with a slight scowl.

"Eliza is English," Jane corrected. "She married a French count."

The Colonel blew his nose loudly into his handkerchief. "I don't hold with our young ladies marrying foreigners in wartime," he said. "It makes for divided loyalties."

Jane felt her temper rising, but was careful to keep her voice measured. "Colonel Waring, my cousin's loyalties to England are clear. She married the Comte more than a decade ago. Besides, she is now a widow. Last year her husband was guillotined by the French Republic!"

Waring's face, bulbous and unattractive at the best of times, turned red. He mumbled an apology.

"I entreat you to take your newspaper back, sir. You can read of true enemies to our nation there, no doubt." Jane pushed herself away from the table and shoved the letter into her pocket.

No sooner had she left the room than she regretted her impertinence. Thank goodness Eliza was coming so that Jane would not have to tolerate Elizabeth and her dull guests alone. Cassandra was no use; she was too polite to have any fun at others' expense. But not Eliza. Recently out of mourning for her poor husband, Eliza would still know all the gossip. And of course her trunks would be full of the latest fashions. Despite the fourteen-year difference in their ages, Jane adored her beautiful and accomplished cousin. She headed for the library; she had an invitation to write.

CHAPTER 2

"How!" cried Elinor; "have you been
repeating to me what you only learnt yourself
by listening at the door? . . . How could
you behave so unfairly by your sister?"
SENSE AND SENSIBILITY

The library was by far Jane's favorite room in the house. There were two fireplaces and ample furniture. She had once counted twenty-eight chairs and five tables. From Edward's desk she took a piece of creamy notepaper from a generous stack—now *this* was true luxury—and settled herself at a table. A trimmed quill pen was ready and the ink was fresh. She drafted a quick invitation to Eliza and then rang for a servant. "Please put this in the next post," she said. The footman took the letter and withdrew as silently as he had arrived.

Jane wandered about the room. The library was fully stocked from floor to ceiling with leather-bound books, but few of them had their spines cracked. As she scanned the shelves she noted there was not a novel published in the last few years to be found, much less Mrs. Radcliffe's latest. That was a pity, but not unexpected. Edward and Elizabeth were not readers.

She selected an illustrated edition of Cowper's poems and settled herself in a high-backed chair in front of the fire at the far end of the library. Without ceremony she propped her feet up on the grate and began to read.

Before she could make much progress, she heard the door open at the other end of the library. She peeked around the back of the chair, fully prepared to remain hidden if the newcomer was unwelcome. It was Edward.

She was about to reveal herself when there was a tapping at the doors to the garden. From behind the chair's wing, Jane watched, curious. Who could be visiting Edward this early? Morning calls weren't made until after lunch, and it was just half past ten.

Edward let in the visitor himself. Jane ducked down further into the chair and drew in her feet.

"Mr. Knight." The visitor's voice was deep and graveled. "Thank you for seeing me so early."

"Major Smythe, have a seat." There was the scraping of chair legs against the parquet floor. "You said it involved a matter of England's security," Edward said. "What does the War Office want with me?"

Jane raised her eyebrows. The War Office was a nebulous term for the men who ran the war and, it was rumored, a vast network of spies and informants. Abroad, its role was to fight foreign enemies, but at home the War Office concerned itself with stemming the spread of radical ideas from France.

After a long pause, Major Smythe said, "It concerns a member of your family."

Edward's voice became less affable. "Which brother?"

"None of them, Mr. Knight."

Both Jane and Edward sighed in relief. Jane covered her mouth with her hand. She must not make a sound.

"I'm speaking of your cousin, the Comtesse de Feuillide."

Jane went very still.

"Eliza?" Edward repeated. "Why on earth would you care about her?"

"We have reason to believe that she is working with the enemy." Major Smythe paused. "That she is a spy for France."

Jane was stunned. Apparently Edward was, too, because he was silent for a long moment. Then he hooted with laughter. "My dear man. Her husband, the Comte, was brutally guillotined not more than a year ago. Why would she help the French? The idea is preposterous!"

"She has been observed visiting a Frenchman, a Mr. Balmont, whom we believe is spying for the French. And we have intercepted communiqués addressed to her that are very suspicious."

"I don't believe it," Edward protested.

"I have the proof right here."

Jane heard the rustle of paper and a half-breathed mumble as Edward read it aloud. "This seems harmless enough," he said, chuckling lightly. "A servant from her husband's estate is asking for money. It's common enough; hardly a threat to our nation's security."

"Or it may be a clever code," the major countered. "We cannot take the risk. The War Office needs your help."

Jane heard the table squeak across the floor as Edward shoved it away from him and got up. Jane pressed herself deep into the chair's upholstery to keep hidden.

"What kind of help?" Edward asked finally, distaste in his voice.

"Invite her here, to Godmersham. You're only twenty miles from the coast. We think it very likely her spymasters won't be able to resist having her collect sensitive information."

"What do you think she has to offer the French? The latest hats here in Kent?"

"The Countess has been traveling among the various port towns—"

"Where she has many friends," Edward interrupted.

"Exactly." Major Smythe spoke as if Edward had conceded the point, not rebutted it. "She may be passing information about our readiness to repel an attack. And we know you are hosting a shooting party next week. Many important military men will be here. I don't have to tell you how easy it is for men to be indiscreet with a beautiful woman."

Slowly, Edward said, "It is not a coincidence that her arrangements were unsettled, is it?"

"No. We prevailed upon her hostess to feign an illness. We hoped she would contact your sister, Miss Jane Austen. Who in turn would invite the Countess here."

Jane frowned. She didn't like being manipulated.

"I do not appreciate my hospitality being abused." Edward's voice was indignant. "Nor do I like inviting my cousin here under false pretenses."

Jane nodded. Despite her brother's recent acquisition of wealth and position, she was relieved to see that he was still loyal to his family.

"No one hopes that more than I. But what if you are wrong, Mr. Knight? How would that look for your family? You have brothers with careers to make in the military. Besides, if my suspicions are correct, in light of the Countess's connection to your family, it could be arranged that the consequences would not be severe."

"You can promise that?" Edward asked.

Jane sighed. Her brother was going to give in.

"Yes. So you'll do it?"

"I believe you are mistaken about Eliza," Edward said. "But as I am sworn to protect England—and for the sake of my family—I will do as you ask."

Jane pressed her knuckles to her lips. She waited for Edward to show Major Smythe out. Then, unable to contain herself, she jumped up, fists clenched at her side.

"Edward, I'm ashamed of you!" she cried.

"Jane, what the devil are you doing there?" Edward shouted.

"Mortified that my own brother should so betray another member of the family. Especially one as sweet and deserving of our trust as Eliza," Jane shot back. "Who among us has suffered as she has?"

Edward's florid face flushed even more with anger and embarrassment. "You're eavesdropping again," he scolded. "It was an irritating habit when you were young; now it is deplorable."

He towered over her, but she tilted her chin up and met his gaze squarely. "I did not intend to eavesdrop, but what was I to do when you and your crony started to malign my dearest cousin?"

Edward's bluster evaporated. He sank into an armchair and looked imploringly at his sister. "You heard everything—do you think Smythe's suspicions could be true?"

"Of course not," Jane insisted. "Eliza would never be a traitor. She is much too frivolous. She couldn't hold a treasonous plot in her head for more than a few minutes. You know her, Edward!"

"He showed me proof." Edward's eyes went to his desk. Before he could stop her, Jane strode over and picked up the letter there. "That's confidential!"

She scanned it quickly. "This is not proof of anything. It's a harmless letter from a servant. It's hardly a state secret."

"You heard Smythe—he thinks it's a code."

"I'm sure your Major Smythe sees conspiracies everywhere. Clearly Eliza's travels, her Continental friends, and her admiration of French fashion have aroused his worst misgivings. But just because he wants this to be an encoded message doesn't make it so. Eliza would no sooner betray England than she would wear last season's gown."

The tension left Edward's face. "I'm sure you're right. She will visit, nothing will happen, and Major Smythe will forget all about her." Edward put his hands on Jane's shoulders and kissed her cheek. "I'll take that letter; it should be locked up."

Reluctant to part with the only evidence against Eliza, Jane handed it to him.

"And I want you to stop prying into other people's affairs," he said over his shoulder as he stowed the letter in his desk. "It's not ladylike. Who'll marry a woman who cannot mind her own business?"

"As if marrying is the sum of my desires!" Jane replied.

"Dear sister, while you're tolerably pretty, you've no fortune." The kindness in his eyes took some of the sting out of his words. "You must hide that wit of yours and behave yourself. I know that Elizabeth has invited some eligible men for you to meet during our shooting party. I had hoped Cassandra would meet someone, too, but she seems set on her curate." Cassandra had an understanding with a poor cleric named Fowle who could not yet afford a wife.

"Cassandra loves her Mr. Fowle and is happy to wait for him," Jane retorted. "I, on the other hand, am in no hurry to yoke my future to someone else's."

"It's high time. How old are you now? Twenty?"

"Nineteen," Jane said, trying to reclaim a little dignity.

"Then I'll have Elizabeth invite a few more gentlemen who can overlook your opinions . . . and your advanced age."

Jane grabbed a pillow from a chair and tossed it at his head. "Get out!" she cried.

"Guard that temper of yours," he teased, wagging a finger at her. When she picked up a book, he protected his head with his arms. Chuckling, Edward retreated from the room.

Jane rushed to the desk, but it was locked tight. Ruefully she admitted to herself that her brother knew her only too well. However, she had an excellent memory. She quickly jotted down the sender's name and the details of the letter.

Tucking her notation in her skirt pocket, she wrote another letter to Eliza. This letter contradicted the first in every particular. *Do not come to Godmersham*, she wrote. Instead she suggested that they meet somewhere nearby and continue on to Steventon together.

Jane rang for the footman. When he glided into the room—how did Elizabeth train them to be so silent?—Jane spoke without ceremony. "That letter I gave you earlier? I'd like it back, please."

A superior look on his face, the footman answered, "It has already been posted, Miss."

"For the first time, I see the disadvantage of having too organized a household," Jane murmured. "Very well; Eliza will just have to pay the postage twice." Since the recipient paid the postage, Jane was usually more considerate with her letter writing, but Eliza's doting godfather had settled a fortune on her, so Jane wasn't overly worried that she was taxing her cousin's purse.

The footman whipped out a silver tray from behind his back and accepted the letter. He turned to leave, but Jane called him back. "By any chance do you know where my sister is?"

"In the nursery, Miss."

"Of course she is." Jane sighed in exasperation.

A flicker of emotion flitted across the footman's face. As Jane left for the nursery, she was sure she saw him struggling to contain a smile.

Jane made her way to the nursery to find Cassandra literally overrun with children. The littlest boy, Harry, was perched on Cassandra's stomach. Jane lifted him off and put him to one side. He started to howl.

Jane knelt down to gaze straight into his eyes. "Harry, do you know what terrible thing happened to the last little boy who cried too much?" she asked solemnly.

His mouth snapped shut. Staring at her, mesmerized, he shook his head.

"He was snatched up by a monster that gnashed his legs between its gigantic teeth like toothpicks before—"

"Jane!" Cassandra scolded.

"Go find your nanny," Jane said. Harry, his eyes wide and terrified, scurried away to the other side of the nursery.

"You should be kinder to the children, Jane," Cassandra said with a sigh.

"Forget the children," Jane snapped. "It is urgent that we talk privately."

She glanced over at the nanny occupied with her charges in the corner.

Cassandra obediently clambered to her feet, dusted off her skirts, and asked, "Whatever is the matter?"

Now that it was time to confide in her sister, Jane wasn't sure what to say. "It may be nothing . . ."

"It's not like you to bewilder me so! What on earth has happened?"

"I overheard something."

Cassandra's delicate eyebrows lifted and came together in a charming scowl. "Jane! Eavesdropping again? It's such a deplorable habit!"

Jane rushed to explain. "I was reading in the library when Edward came in. He had a clandestine meeting in the library with a stranger who came in by way of the garden. Of course I had to listen. Wouldn't you?"

"No."

"Well, that may be. But you are always happy to hear what I have uncovered!" Jane pulled her armchair closer to her sister and leaned her dark head near Cassandra's fair cheek.

As Jane whispered what she had heard, she was gratified to watch Cassandra's puzzlement turn to outrage. "That is the most absurd thing I've ever heard!" Cassandra cried. "Eliza is a true Englishwoman. What does it matter if she prefers French food? You didn't credit this accusation for an instant, did you?"

"Of course not," Jane hurriedly reassured her.

"Besides," Cassandra continued, "Eliza has spent more time in England nursing her mother and caring for her son than she ever spent in France. Poor Hastings requires all her attention. She wouldn't have any time to spy for France, even if she had the inclination!"

"And she would never help the regime that has made her a widow," Jane finished.

"What can we do?" Cassandra asked.

Jane took Cassandra's hands in hers. She couldn't help but notice how spotless they were compared with her own ink-stained fingers. "I've already written to Eliza, warning her not to come."

"Did you tell her why?"

"Not in a letter. As Eliza will have to learn, our private correspondence is not as secure as we would like. I simply said I would prefer to meet her somewhere else. But I made the letter as mysterious as possible to be sure she pays attention."

"But we've only just arrived!"

"I won't lure Eliza here for Edward and his spies in the War Office."

"Does our brother know your plan?"

"Of course not. Edward has no gift for spycraft," Jane said. "But since you shall remain, you can report to me anything Edward reveals, however inadvertently. I doubt that our correspondence is important enough to be intercepted, so our secrets should be safe."

Cassandra tilted her head and regarded her younger sister. "But Edward won't let you hire a coach by yourself." It was a perpetual problem. The Austen sisters often had invitations to visit one house or another, but their male relations forbade them to travel without an escort.

Jane frowned for a moment and then dismissed the problem with a wave. "I'll think of something."

CHAPTER 3

*"There is a stubbornness about me that
never can bear to be frightened at the
will of others. My courage always rises
at every attempt to intimidate me."*
PRIDE AND PREJUDICE

*J*ane received another letter the next day while the
family and their guests were sitting in the drawing room
before dinner. The late-afternoon sun was fading and the
servants were starting to light the expensive wax candles.
Edward and Elizabeth had their dinner at the fashionably
late hour of five o'clock. At home, the Austens ate while
there was still natural light to see by. Cassandra was

showing Elizabeth her sketches of the children, while Jane read her book of poems. The footman presented the letter first to Elizabeth, who waved him toward Jane.

Edward was watchful as Jane broke the wax seal on the letter. She met his eyes briefly over the top of the paper and then silently read Eliza's words, scrawled large with no regard for economy of paper or ink.

Ma chère Jane,

Quel mystère délicieux. First you invite me to the finest château in Kent, then in the same day you not only rescind the invitation, but insist we must rendezvous elsewhere! How delightfully secretive.

I will wait for you at Sevenoaks. It is not so far from London nor Godmersham. There is a pleasant inn there, the Fox and Hounds. I will send my carriage to fetch you demain après-midi. Jacques, my coachman, is an excellent driver and will conduct you here in perfect safety.

À bientôt!

Eliza

Eliza's curiosity was gratifying and ensured that she would do as Jane asked. Given the circumstances, Jane would have preferred her cousin restrain her liberal use of French phrases, but Eliza had affected such mannerisms for too long to change now.

Suddenly aware of the silence in the room, Jane looked up to see everyone's eyes on her.

"Is it from your dear cousin?" Elizabeth asked eagerly. "When will she be coming?"

"Yes, Jane, when?" Edward asked, suspicion in his eyes.

"Unfortunately, Eliza must decline your kind invitation," Jane said, watching her brother. "She is still overcome with grief from the sad business of her husband's death. She prefers to go to Steventon, where she can retreat from all society."

"Nonsense," Edward said. "If she is melancholy, your company is the surest antidote."

Jane glanced triumphantly at Cassandra. "Dear Edward, I am so glad you think so. Even though I have only just arrived at Godmersham, I feel it is my duty to go to my cousin and be her comfort."

"But . . . that's not what I meant!" Edward babbled.

Elizabeth frowned, her thoughts as apparent as if she had written them down. If the Comtesse was unavailable, then Elizabeth could very well spare Jane. "But what about Cassandra?" Elizabeth asked.

"I will stay, of course," Cassandra assured her.

With a relieved smile, Elizabeth took up her embroidery. "Good. We cannot do without her!" Without much interest, she asked, "Jane, when will you go?"

"Tomorrow."

"Nonsense!" Edward nearly shouted. "I cannot spare the carriage, and I won't allow you to travel by post chaise alone." He folded his arms smugly across his chest.

Carefully folding Eliza's letter and placing it in her pocket, Jane looked at her brother. "Happily, I do not need to impose upon you or your carriage. Eliza is sending hers for me."

The next day, precisely at noon, Eliza's carriage arrived. Jane followed its progress through the park from the bedroom window.

"Perfect," Jane said, pointing the fine carriage out to her sister. "No fewer than four horses. Even Edward will have nothing to complain about."

"I wish I were going with you," Cassandra said.

Jane lifted her eyebrows. "You hate adventure. Your preference is always to be in front of a warm fire."

Cassandra shrugged her shoulders and smiled.

"Besides," Jane continued, "you must stay here and find out as much as you can. Edward won't suspect *you* of ulterior motives."

"Unlike you, I have no hidden depths," Cassandra said. "I seem scrupulous because I am."

"But you shall be all the more guileful for that," Jane assured her.

After she said her goodbyes to Cassandra, Jane went down the main staircase, Mervyn the footman following behind with her trunk. Elizabeth was indisposed after lunch, sparing Jane the effort of saying farewell, but Edward was waiting at the front door.

"Jane," he began. "I am your older brother, and I must forbid you to go."

Jane stared at him for a few moments until he looked abashed. "I can make my own decisions," she said lightly.

With a glance at the footman, Edward drew her to an alcove in the main hall. "Jane, I know you are responsible for Eliza's change of plans. You must bring her here so I can clear her name."

"Dear brother, you half-believe she is guilty. I do not. Which of us is better suited to help her?"

"You are meddling in affairs that are bigger than yourself. It is dangerous," he warned.

"I won't be used to lure Eliza into a trap, brother. I'll solve this problem on my own—without your Major Smythe."

"Then perhaps I should come to Steventon?"

"And what of your very important guests?" Jane asked mischievously. "They are expecting a shooting party."

"Blast the guests. This is family business," he said.

"Father is at Oxford, but Mother would be delighted to see you. She often says that since you came into your inheritance, you never visit."

"That's unfair. I've got so much to do on the estate . . ." he began before he realized she was mocking him. "Stop teasing, Jane. Very well, I'll let you go. But take care, please? I don't think there's anything to this story of Eliza being a spy, but there must be something going on to arouse Smythe's suspicions."

"He struck me as a most mistrustful sort of person."

"That's his job," Edward said. "Are you sure you will be all right going alone?"

"Eliza's coachman, Jacques, will take excellent care of me," she assured him.

"Jacques? He's *French*?" Edward was clearly appalled.

"All of Eliza's servants are. They all come from her husband's estate. And trust me, they are all very loyal to her."

"Be careful," he repeated.

"I shall. Thank you for your hospitality, although I didn't take advantage of it for very long."

"You are always welcome here," he said.

"Thank you, dear brother. If it were up to you, I'm sure that would be true."

"Elizabeth means well . . ."

Jane put her hand to her brother's cheek. "It's fine, Edward."

Edward nodded as they stepped to the carriage. "Please take care, Jane." He handed her a parcel he had waiting at the door. "This is for you," he said.

Pleased, she accepted the package. "Is it writing paper?" His indulgent smile told her the answer. Impulsively, she threw her arms around his neck. "Thank you, Edward!" Then before any further displays of affection could embarrass her, Jane turned to go outside.

Jacques was waiting respectfully. He had already stowed Jane's trunk, whose shabbiness was an embarrassment to the elegant vehicle.

His face was round and dark and perfectly inscrutable, as a good servant's should be. His only unusual characteristic was a shock of brown hair that stood up from the back of his head. As soon as Jane appeared he hurried to open the door to the carriage.

The carriage was even more luxurious inside than out. The dark red velvet seats were plush and thick, to cushion the traveler against ruts in the road. Jacques had put heated bricks in felt pockets on the floor so her toes would stay warm. Trust Eliza to travel in comfort.

Jane looked through the narrow rectangle of glass behind her head. She caught a glimpse of the window of their room, but Cassandra was gone, conscripted no doubt to help with the children. Jane gave a quick wave to Edward and sat back in her comfortable seat.

With a shake of the reins, the carriage lurched forward. Jane was off for a rendezvous with adventure. She could not recall looking forward to anything quite so much. But Godmersham was not long behind them when Jacques opened the small window that let the driver communicate with his passengers.

"Mademoiselle Austen, I fear we are being followed."

CHAPTER 4

*This sort of mysteriousness, which is
always so becoming in a hero . . . increased
her anxiety to know more of him.*
NORTHANGER ABBEY

*J*ane scrambled to her knees to peer out the back window. Even though it was still early afternoon, the road was deserted—not a farmer or wagon to be seen for miles, just a solitary horseman charging toward them. He was several hundred feet behind the carriage, but he was gaining.

Jane's heart skipped a beat; her brothers were always warning her about bandits who preyed on innocent travelers. It would be too aggravating to have to admit that Edward had been right.

"Hold tight, mademoiselle." Jacques cracked his whip and the carriage lurched forward.

Bracing herself against the jolting, Jane fixed her eyes on the rider. As he urged his steed faster, Jane saw he wore a dark black cape and hat. He drew closer, and she saw that he had draped a scarlet scarf about his face, hiding his features. Her fingers tightened on the windowsill. She was breathing so quickly she felt lightheaded. "Make haste, Jacques!" she shouted.

In another moment, the horseman drew abreast of the carriage horses and pointed a pistol at Jacques.

"Stop the carriage," the bandit shouted.

Jacques ignored him and whipped the horses to greater speed.

"Stop the carriage!" the bandit shouted again as he fired the pistol in the air. His horse, frothing at the bit from its exertions, reared. Rounding a turn, the carriage tipped, the wheels on the right side leaving the ground. Jane was thrown against the side of the carriage and then fell to the floor. She squeezed her eyes tight, waiting for the crash, but with a terrible thud the carriage wheels slammed back onto the road. Jacques shouted at the horses and cracked his whip.

"Jacques, do as he says!" Jane shouted as loudly as she could. "Stop, Jacques! Arrêtez!" If the choice were to be crushed in a carriage accident or to face an armed bandit, she would take her chances with the bandit.

Jacques pulled the horses to a stop. Jane climbed back to her seat and breathed deeply, forcing herself to be calm.

Outside the carriage, the man reined in his horse. Carefully replacing his pistol in a holster at his belt, he called out. "Madame, I apologize for my brusqueness. I sincerely pray that you suffered no injury. I meant no discourtesy, but I had no other way to beg an audience. Come out of the carriage, s'il vous plaît."

Straining to hear every word, Jane peeked out the window. Disbelief warred with relief in her mind. The gunman didn't sound like a criminal. Perhaps he was a gentleman-bandit, such as one read about in one of Mrs. Radcliffe's novels? Jane couldn't believe her luck to actually meet one.

I am not afraid, she told herself. She adjusted her bonnet and straightened her gloves. She stepped outside. The wind was sharp and sliced through her woolen pelisse.

She lifted her chin to consider her pursuer. His clothes showed signs of hard travel and long wear, but she could see that they had originally been tailored and expensive. A gentleman-bandit indeed.

"Mademoiselle!" he said, surprise evident in his voice. "Please ask the Comtesse de Feuillide to join us."

"And if I decline?" she asked. "Would you shoot me?"

"I would much prefer not to," he said in a genial manner.

"You are no bandit," she said, contemplating his appearance and demeanor. "Perhaps you are a French émigré fallen upon hard times?"

"Very hard times," he agreed. Above the disguising scarf, his eyes were dark brown with flecks of gold. "I shall ask again: Please have the Comtesse de Feuillide step outside."

"I am alone," Jane said matter-of-factly, although the words made her realize how vulnerable she was. Jacques was perched high on the carriage seat, and what could he do to protect her from a pistol?

"This is the Comtesse's carriage, is it not?" he said, gesturing toward the crest on the door behind Jane. It was newly painted in gold and proclaimed to anyone with a knowledge of heraldry that this was the de Feuillide carriage.

"Yes, it is. But I assure you I am its only occupant."

The man dismounted, strode past her, and threw open the carriage door. "Where is she?" he demanded, turning to Jane.

"I am not accustomed to being interrogated by strangers who are armed," she said, watching him carefully. He was of medium height and medium build. His hands were gloved so she could see no identifying ring. Even his hair was hidden under his sweeping hat. Was there nothing to distinguish him except those gold-speckled eyes?

He paused, and then bowed slightly from his waist in the Continental fashion. "I must apologize for my ill manners. Would you be so good as to tell me where I could find the Comtesse?"

A mysterious Frenchman was looking for Eliza. Jane felt a prickling of anxiety. Perhaps the rumors were true and Eliza had allied herself with the French. But if that were so, this stranger would not have to act the highwayman and force her vehicle to stop. He must be Eliza's enemy despite his elegant manners. Therefore, he was Jane's enemy as well.

These thoughts took no longer than an instant. "Perhaps I could carry a message to the Comtesse?" she suggested.

He shook his head. "I think not, mademoiselle. I have no wish to detain you further; just tell me where to find the Comtesse, and you may be on your way."

"I shall not tell you where the Comtesse is, and I shall be on my way regardless," Jane said, growing more confident with every exchange that the man would not harm her. "If she welcomed your company, then you would already know how to find her."

He hesitated, and then cursed. Jane's French was rudimentary, but with six brothers, she could recognize profanity in several languages.

The mysterious man mounted his horse. Pulling in the reins tightly, he looked down on her. "The Comtesse has a staunch ally in her cousin. I suspect we shall meet again, Miss Austen."

"Wait," Jane cried, stepping toward him. "How do you know my name?"

He bowed his head and touched his fingers to his hat and then to his lips. Then he kicked his horse and galloped away.

Jane stood in the center of the road, watching him go. She did not believe he had given up. No doubt, he would wait for them farther along the road and follow them from there.

Jacques climbed down the ladder so rapidly he almost fell. "Mademoiselle, are you all right? I didn't know what to do."

She held up a reassuring hand. "He did not hurt me. You did the correct thing."

They both stared after the horseman, who was growing smaller in the distance. "Did you recognize him?" she asked.

"How should I know a highwayman? Because we are both French?" he bristled. "I am loyal, both to my mistress and to my adopted country."

"Jacques, I wasn't questioning your loyalty. Consult your memory. Was that gentleman—and despite his actions I do not think he was a highwayman—familiar to you in any way? Perhaps he was an associate of the late Comte?"

Jacques shrugged. "I do not know him, mademoiselle."

"But he knew my name!" Jane said. "He must be some-one with whom I am acquainted." She searched her memory, but she couldn't recall meeting anyone like the stranger. Of course, he had carefully hidden anything that might identify him. But what about that odd gesture at the end? Was it French? Or was it unique to him?

To better remember the movement, she mimicked it, her fingers going to her forehead, then briefly touching her lips.

Jacques started. "Mademoiselle, forgive my impertinence, but why did you do that?"

"The mysterious gentleman did it as he took his leave. Didn't you see?"

He shook his head.

"You've seen it before!" Jane accused. "What does it mean?"

"Rien. For an instant . . . but no. C'est impossible." Jacques simply shook his head. "We must resume our journey, mademoiselle. La Comtesse will be waiting." He held the door open for her.

"But, Jacques . . ."

The perfectly blank expression on the servant's face told Jane that ask as she might, she'd get no further information from him. Suddenly, Jane wanted very much to see Eliza.

CHAPTER 5

"You do not look well. Oh that I had
been with you! You have had every care
and anxiety upon yourself alone."
PRIDE AND PREJUDICE

*J*ane could barely sit still until they arrived at the Fox and Hounds. Her body hummed with an excitement she'd never felt before. She felt so alive. Jane had often written about adventures in her stories, but this was the first time she was the heroine of her own. With a self-deprecating sigh, she amended the thought. She was the heroine of this particular tale solely because of a mistaken identity.

They pulled up in front of the Fox and Hounds Inn. Without waiting for Jacques to open the door, Jane flew out of the carriage into the inn, past the curious eyes of the hostler. She went to the reception desk and asked for Eliza. Upon being directed to a private room in the restaurant, she hurried there. Without ceremony, she threw open the door.

Eliza was dozing in a comfortable chair by the fire. When the door slammed against the wall, she jumped, her illustrated newspaper sliding to the floor. She blinked and then squinted. Her eyesight was poor, but she was too vain to admit it.

"Who's there?" Eliza called.

Jane rushed to her cousin.

"Jane?" Eliza yawned delicately. She shook her head to wake herself up, setting the bonnet covering her powdered curls askew. "What on earth is wrong with you? First you write the most perplexing letters, and now you burst in like a summer storm."

Jane gathered her wits, reminding herself that if Eliza were innocent, then she knew of no reason to be concerned. "I apologize, dear Eliza."

"Perhaps you are just tired. You must refresh yourself after your journey." Before Jane could protest, Eliza rang a bell and the inn's serving girl appeared. "A basin of warm water for my cousin, please?"

"Yes, ma'am." The servant stared at Eliza with near adoration. Jane never understood how Eliza could give servants as much trouble as she did but remain everyone's favorite.

"Where is Marie?" Jane asked. Marie was Eliza's maid and was always in attendance.

"My pelisse had an unfortunate encounter with some mud on the journey. She's attempting to rescue it," Eliza explained.

A few minutes later, Jane's coat had been neatly put away and she had bathed her face. Eliza pressed a glass of mulled wine into her hand. "Maintenant dis-moi, ma chérie, what happened?"

"There was a frightening incident on the road today. I feared for your safety."

"*My* safety?" Eliza's plucked eyebrows lifted in surprise. "Jane, have you been drinking? Perhaps your brother gave you a flask of brandy to warm you on the journey?"

Jane shook her head. Edward would never think to give his sister spirits no matter how long the trip. She took a deep breath. "We were waylaid by an armed man on horseback." Her matter-of-fact tone didn't stop her heart from beating more quickly at the memory.

Eliza sat up and gasped. "A highwayman? Near here?"

"Yes, less than an hour ago," Jane answered. Quickly, she related her adventure.

"And he was looking for me?" Eliza marveled. Jane watched her closely, looking for clues that Eliza might know very well who the mysterious stranger was.

"Does he sound familiar?" Jane asked. "He knew I was your cousin—that implies some knowledge of your connections."

Eliza frowned prettily. "Do you really think I have so many masked men among my acquaintance? I know no one so eccentric. Why not just call upon me? Or send a letter?"

Knowing that letters to Eliza were liable to be intercepted, Jane wondered whether the masked man was prudent rather than dangerous.

"Jane, what else is there?" Eliza, for all her affectation, was quite shrewd. Her eyes narrowed and she jabbed a finger in Jane's direction. "What haven't you told me?"

Edward had not sworn Jane to secrecy, which was his mistake. Jane didn't hesitate. "My brother Edward has been charged to keep a watchful eye on you."

"By whom?" Eliza's enormous eyes went wide, reflecting the dancing flames from the fireplace.

"The War Office."

"The War Office is interested in me?" Eliza's hand went to her bosom. "But why?"

Jane hesitated. "They suspect you of . . . well . . ."

"Out with it, Jane! I've never once known you to hold your peace—can you be so exasperating as to begin now?"

"Espionage."

Eliza's face was so full of puzzlement that now Jane was sure the intelligence was news to her. "They think you are sending information to the French government about our troops and port defenses," Jane said softly.

Eliza was motionless as a china doll. When she spoke, her voice was full of indignation. "The French Republic has made me a widow. Why would I help them?" She pulled off her fashionable bonnet. Jane caught her breath. Instead of the long curls that fell below Eliza's shoulder, her cousin's hair was only a few inches long.

"What have you done to your hair?" Jane asked, appalled. She herself kept her hair short, to her shoulder, but only because it was less trouble. Eliza had a maid, and her hairdressing was always ornate.

"This is what a woman looks like before the guillotine." Eliza's hand went to a tendril of hair lying against her cheek. "They cut Marie Antoinette's hair like this before they took her head. The same guillotine killed Jean. So I decided I'll wear my hair like this until his death is avenged."

Jane nodded. Only four years had passed since England had been shocked by the murder of King Louis XVI. A few months later, his queen had lost her head as well. Eliza's husband of fourteen years, the Comte de Feuillide, had been executed the following year for being loyal to the deposed monarchy. Eliza had lost her husband, and her son had lost his birthright, including his title and the estate in France.

Jane reached out and took Eliza's hands in her own. Edward and his friend Major Smythe were fools to think that Eliza would aid the French.

"Besides," Eliza said, "short hair is all the rage among the émigrés!"

Jane couldn't help but smile. Her cousin's vanity would always trump politics.

"Troops and ports are ridiculously dull," Eliza mused. "Even if I knew anything about them, I would do my best to forget as quickly as possible."

"That's what Cassandra and I thought as well," Jane agreed. "But apparently there are concerns about the company you keep. It has been noted that you have been a frequent guest at the home of a Mr. Balmont in London."

"But of course. I knew Monsieur Balmont first in Paris. I renewed the acquaintance here in England. His chef is the best in London; an invitation to one of Monsieur Balmont's suppers is much sought after."

"Edward has been told that Mr. Balmont is a well-known spymaster for the French."

"So?" Eliza blinked her bright eyes and shrugged. "That does not affect the quality of his meals."

Jane settled back in her chair, arms crossed. "Eliza, for an instant, please be serious. Your association with this man is damaging your reputation."

"Only among the bores who run the War Office," Eliza said, stretching her hands out to the fireplace. "But in any case Monsieur Balmont's salon is full of émigrés—all of London is. You cannot walk across Pall Mall without meeting an acquaintance from Marie Antoinette's court. Did I ever tell you about the time the queen came to a ball dressed as a Turk and covered with feathers and diamonds?"

Jane held up an impatient hand. "That is ancient history, Eliza. Pray listen to me. The English government is particularly interested in you." She hesitated, then said, "They are watching your every move. They have intercepted at least one of your letters and found it very suspicious."

"They're reading my mail?" Eliza frowned. "But I don't recall receiving any suspicious letters."

"They kept the letter," Jane said. "I saw it."

"Jane, how am I supposed to know anything about a letter that I never received?" Eliza exclaimed.

"It is possible that I might have scribbled down some of the details of my best recollection of the letter," Jane admitted, pulling the paper from her pocket. She and Eliza pored over it. "It was from a former servant in France. He said he had fallen upon hard times and needed your assistance. If not intercepted, the letter would have reached you six weeks ago. You were in London then, weren't you?"

Eliza nodded. "Yes. Hastings had several doctor's appointments."

Hastings was Eliza's son. He was eight years old, but had the intellectual capacity of a child half his age. He had problems with his balance and could barely walk. No doctor had ever been able to cure his malady. Eliza doted on him.

"How is Hastings?" Jane asked.

"He was not well enough to travel. I left him in London with his governess. Travel stimulates his mind entirely too much."

"Mother will be disappointed; she adores Hastings," Jane said, and was rewarded by Eliza's indulgent smile. Eliza liked nothing better than to hear her son praised.

"So you were in London when this was written?" Jane asked, returning to the subject.

"Yes. But I never received that letter. Tell me, Jane, do you know the name of the servant who wrote it?"

"A servant named René Geroux."

"René?" Eliza exclaimed. "That is impossible. He's dead."

At that moment, the door swung open and Marie came in with a tray of sweets. "Madame," she said. "The innkeeper wishes to know if we intend to stay the night or continue on."

Jane reflected that only a woman as confident as Eliza could have a maid who was so pretty. Younger than her mistress, Marie had the face of an angel, with thick dark hair and black eyes.

"Jane, what do you think? Should we go now?"

"Steventon is at least seventy miles away. If we try to go now, we'll be traveling in the dark and will have to break our journey overnight anyway."

Eliza nodded. "Not to mention the highwayman might be waiting!"

Marie's face reflected her alarm. "Madame?"

"Don't worry, Marie," Eliza reassured her. "We will go tomorrow. Tell Jacques, s'il te plaît."

After Marie had left, Eliza said, "Promise me you will not mention any of this spy business in front of Marie. The highwayman she will hear about from Jacques—but the rest must be between us. Particularly the letter."

Jane regarded her cousin. "Why especially the letter?" she asked.

"René was her husband. She and I were widowed by the same guillotine."

CHAPTER 6

"From you, from my home, I shall never again
have the smallest incitement to move . . ."
SENSE AND SENSIBILITY

*J*ane was exceedingly glad to be home. Entering the drawing room, she sighed in satisfaction. The parsonage at Steventon was exceedingly plain and modest compared to her brother's home—compared to any domicile of substance—but she liked its simplicity. The beams might be exposed and the furniture sparse, but it was an honest house.

In past years the noise of six brothers, two sisters, and Mr. Austen's boarding students had filled the rooms. Since the sons were all now launched in their careers and only the two daughters remained at home, Jane's father had recently decided that he no longer needed to tutor students. Now the house echoed with emptiness.

This particular morning, Jane's mother was ensconced on the sofa to one side of the fire. Mrs. Austen had long been known throughout the county for her efficient management of a large family, their boarders, her poultry farm, and the parsonage, all on a limited income. Now, at long last, Mrs. Austen could indulge herself and nurse a head cold.

Mr. Austen was detained at Oxford and would not return for several days. The only brother at home for a visit was James, Jane's oldest brother. He was out shooting; the fine weather had extended the shooting season well into January.

Jane settled herself at her writing desk, the perfect distance from the fire. Her father had given the desk to her for Christmas, and it was by far the nicest gift she had ever received.

"When will Eliza come down?" Mrs. Austen asked in a querulous voice. "It's almost noon!"

"I believe she's still asleep," Jane explained. "Our journey was fatiguing." *But thankfully uneventful*, she thought. There had been no sign of the masked man during the ride home.

Much as Jane had wanted to, she and Eliza were not able to discuss him, constrained as they were by the presence of Marie the maid. "Eliza is not used to our country hours."

Mrs. Austen sniffed, putting her handkerchief to her runny nose. "She's already missed breakfast. Prudence will have to bring her a tray; it's very inconvenient for the servants."

Jane blotted the paper in front of her. Growing up in such a crowded house, she had learned to write amidst any distraction. Despite her mother's twittering, she had already managed to begin a new story. The heroine of this story was destined to marry for affection and still enjoy a lavish lifestyle to which she had not been born. And possibly a rogue with a French accent might make an appearance, just to complicate the plot.

"We have no one here to amuse Eliza," her mother went on. "The boys are all away."

"James is here," Jane said, only half of her attention devoted to her mother.

"That's true. Last night he stayed with the Bigg-Withers so they could play cards. But James is hardly likely to exert himself to entertain his widowed cousin. He finds talking to women so difficult. If only his Anne hadn't died!"

James was a clergyman like Jane's father. The year before his wife had died unexpectedly. He had been greatly grieved by the loss, and it reinforced his tendency to be a bit solemn. Jane thought it was about time he was in society again.

"Eliza is very good at frivolity," Jane suggested. "If anyone can teach James to be more lighthearted, it is she."

"Do you think that he and Eliza might make a match of it?" Mrs. Austen asked, sitting up, suddenly alert. "I must say I hadn't thought of it."

"I was joking," Jane assured her. "Our James has many excellent qualities—sobriety, solemnity, piety—and not one of them is likely to attract Eliza's attention other than as an affectionate cousin."

Mrs. Austen sighed. "Perhaps you are right. But then what is Eliza to do while she's here? All of our neighbors are in London for the winter. Except for dear Madame Lefroy, of course. But there is hardly anyone else to distract her. I wonder that she wants to visit us at all."

Jane smiled as she dipped her pen in the ink bottle. "Our cousin is much sought after. She chose to be with us, knowing full well our rustic ways."

"She did indeed, and then came earlier than we expected. Naturally, I was delighted to see you both, but it was a surprise. And why didn't Cassandra join you?"

"My sister could not be spared by our dear sister-in-law," Jane said dryly. "A governess and nurse are not sufficient to amuse Elizabeth's children."

"You should be less judgmental," Mrs. Austen scolded. "It was very kind of Edward to have you at Godmersham. How else are you to be introduced to eligible men? The pickings in Hampshire are quite slim, especially since you are so particular."

Jane's pen nib nearly snapped from the pressure she placed on it. "Mother, the young men in Kent are no more interesting than the men in Hampshire! I wish you would stop assuming that it is everyone's proper job to provide your daughters the opportunity to meet bachelors."

"You pretend it doesn't matter, Jane, but you know better. With such a small fortune as you possess, it would be wise for you to display less intelligence and more beauty if you wish to find a good match."

"I would not want a husband who valued my appearance more than my wit." Jane's response fell into a well-worn groove; she and her mother had had this conversation many times before.

"At least Cassandra is soon to be settled." The partial satisfaction in Mrs. Austen's pronouncement was apparent to Jane. Unsaid was, "What a relief that at least one of my daughters will be married."

But Jane wondered whether Cassandra was really better off. Married to her Mr. Fowle, she would always be scrimping and making economies, since he was even poorer than the Austens. And once Cassandra had children, how were they to manage? Her mind recoiled at the idea of her precious sister bearing child after child, like Edward's wife. Childbearing was dangerous, and she'd rather have a spinster sister than lose Cassandra to anything but old, old age.

"Is it better for Cassandra to be engaged to a poor man?" Jane asked wickedly. "Or should she hold out for someone with a greater fortune?" She pulled out a knife and began to trim her pen.

"Your father and I want nothing more for you girls than happiness," her mother rejoined. "Cassandra will not have a comfortable life unless Mr. Fowle finds a patron. However, she is in love with him. Therefore, we are content for her to wait. But what can we expect from you? No suitor can meet your standards." Mrs. Austen mimicked Jane's voice perfectly. "'Not ten thousand pounds would convince me that his opinions are interesting.' Or 'Rich and handsome, yes, but with vulgar tastes in literature and music.' I despair that you will ever give a gentleman a chance to prove his worth before you judge him wanting."

"Enough, Mother!" Jane said with asperity, replacing the knife in its drawer. "I will try to be more accommodating. I shall set my cap at the next eligible young man—no matter his breeding, his fortune, or his intelligence."

"If only you would, Jane dear." The long-suffering sigh made Jane smile as she scratched her pen to a blank piece of paper. She owed Edward her gratitude for this at least—his parcel of paper would last her for months. She might even dedicate her next story to him.

The doorbell clanged.

"Who can be calling so early?" Mrs. Austen wondered.

"Perhaps that is my future beau now." Jane laughed.

Their maid, Prudence, poked her head in the doorway. "It is Mrs. Lefroy, ma'am. Are you receiving callers?"

Jane leapt up, forestalling her mother from arising from her chair by the fire. "To Madame Lefroy, we are always at home!" Jane exclaimed. "Prudence, show her in."

Madame Lefroy was the wife of the rector at Ashe, a house just a few miles away. Madame was a poet, a great reader, and a beautiful woman. To Jane she embodied the perfect combination of sense and sensibility. The entire district admired her wit and accomplishments, hence her honorary title of "Madame." Her home was always welcoming to her friends, who much appreciated her willingness to throw open the folding doors between her drawing and dining rooms and get up an impromptu dance with five or ten couples of her close acquaintance. She was a particular friend of Jane's despite the difference in their ages: Madame's oldest child, Lucy, was only a few years younger than Jane.

When Madame Lefroy entered the drawing room, her charm brightened the plain room. As always, her hair was beautifully arranged and powdered, yet still appropriate for the country in the dead of winter.

Jane joyfully embraced her friend. After a proper greeting to Mrs. Austen, Madame clasped Jane's hands and exclaimed, "How delightful to see you so soon. We didn't look for you in Hampshire for several more weeks."

Jane explained that her cousin's change of plans had demanded her early return.

"So the famous Comtesse has arrived?" Madame asked, an enigmatic smile playing on her lips. Madame was confident of her standing in the neighborhood, but surely she didn't relish a rival who had not only the advantage of fortune but also the romantic aura of having lost a husband to La Guillotine.

"You will adore her, Madame," Jane assured her. "She is charming."

"If you say so, it must be true," Madame replied generously. She stood in front of the fire, rubbing her chilled arms. "In any event, I am terribly relieved that you are home!"

"Dear Madame Lefroy, I'm always eager to be of use to you," Jane said. "What is troubling you?"

"I have a visitor," Madame explained, with a grimace.

"From your expression, I venture to guess an unwelcome one?" Jane asked.

"Mr. Tom Lefroy. He is my husband's nephew. Only twenty years old, he has the pretensions of someone at least twenty-one."

From her brocaded chair near the fire, Mrs. Austen's interest was clearly piqued at the mention of a young man. "Pray, Madame, tell us about him," she implored.

"He is to study law in London under the tutelage of my husband's uncle, the judge. But after only a month in Town, he's already fallen in with an undesirable group of young men. The judge decided he would do better in the country, getting to know his relations for a few weeks." She turned to face Jane and held out her hands to show her helplessness. "But he is a difficult guest."

"Is he so hard to please?" Jane asked sympathetically.

Madame nodded vehemently. "After ten days, we have exhausted every topic of conversation, and now he says there is nothing interesting to talk about in the country. The hunting has not been as good as he's seen at home. He's not interested in visiting because the young ladies of the district are provincial and dull."

Slyly, Mrs. Austen said, "Jane, he sounds like your ideal match!"

Jane felt her cheeks pinken and hurried to say, "Madame, how can I help?"

Madame Lefroy confided, "I've told him how you and Cassandra are the prettiest girls in the district—and clever besides. He is doubtful, of course, in a particularly smug manner."

"He sounds absolutely irresistible!" Jane remarked.

"I am looking forward to watching you put him in his place."

"Me?" Jane asked.

"That sounds more like Jane," Mrs. Austen said acidly.

"Best of all would be if you could make him fall in love with you, Jane," Madame implored.

Jane burst out laughing. "Why on earth would I do that?" She paused, reconsidered, and added, "Assuming I could, of course."

"Of course you could! Trust me, he would be a terrible match for you for so many reasons—but then you could rebuff him and teach him a lesson."

Mrs. Austen snorted in disgust. "The two of you do not take the business of matrimony seriously. Jane has enough obstacles to a good marriage without you encouraging her to be difficult."

Jane grinned broadly. "Madame, I look forward to the challenge."

The doorbell rang again. Before the maid could announce him, a young man dressed in the latest style for young dandies in London with a well-cut coat and a blindingly white silk shirt appeared in the doorway to the drawing room.

"There you are, Aunt," he said. "I looked around at home and you had disappeared." He tossed his hat and gloves on a settee. Mrs. Austen smoothed her hair and cast a nervous look at her youngest daughter.

"I couldn't wait another moment to see my friends." Madame Lefroy gestured gracefully to the ladies. "Mrs. Austen, Miss Jane Austen, let me present my husband's nephew, Mr. Tom Lefroy."

Mr. Lefroy clicked his heels and Jane curtsied. His face was well formed, but there was an indulged look to his well-shaped lips that to Jane's eye indicated a spoiled temperament. Jane smiled. She was going to enjoy herself.

CHAPTER 7

Elinor was not inclined, after a little
observation, to give him credit for being
so genuinely and unaffectedly ill-natured
or ill-bred as he wished to appear.
SENSE AND SENSIBILITY

"*Y*ou are most welcome in our home, sir!" Mrs. Austen called from her chair. "I'm terribly sorry that I am indisposed. My daughter Jane will have to act as your hostess. She will fill the role admirably, I am sure."

"I am sorry to hear of your indisposition, ma'am," Mr. Lefroy said politely but with little interest. Jane heard a lilt in his words she could not quite place.

"I'm sorry too, Mrs. Austen," Madame said. "What is the nature of your malady?"

"A dreadful cold in my head," Mrs. Austen replied mournfully. "It has quite exhausted me."

"Perhaps we should return another time," Madame said politely.

"Not at all," Jane said. Then she indicated two rather uncomfortable chairs and said, "Please, sit down."

With an air of boredom he did little to disguise, Tom Lefroy took a seat. Mrs. Austen asked him about his stay and if he had been to Ashe or even to Hampshire before. His answers were seldom more than a syllable.

While her mother interrogated this future prospect with utterly predictable questions, Jane observed him closely. He looked about the room as if he were valuing its contents and finding them wanting. He took his watch from his waistcoat and compared its time with the grandfather clock in the corner of the room. Madame watched him with a slight tightening of her mouth, and Jane deduced that this was a fair sample of his manners.

To please her friend, rather than from any desire to converse with him, Jane asked whether Mr. Lefroy was enjoying his time in Hampshire. "Tolerably," he replied with a bored shrug. Jane had seen this mannerism before from London friends her brothers brought home. They enjoyed the novelty of country life for a few days, but then longed for the excitement and society of London.

Mrs. Austen asked, "How long are you staying?"

"My London uncle wants me to stay for another fortnight," he said.

"Are your wishes of no account?" Jane asked sweetly.

"I beg your pardon?" he asked, apparently surprised that Jane had said something unexpected.

"I wondered whether a stay at Ashe Rectory was your preference as well, or whether you were simply accommodating your uncle."

Perhaps her impertinence inspired his gentlemanly instincts. He inclined his head to Madame and said, "No one could find visiting my aunt to be a burden. I must admit, however, that the neighborhood does seem rather quiet. If I weren't able to hunt, I'd be terribly bored."

"There's a frost in the air today. So long as it doesn't snow, the hunting may continue," Mrs. Austen said.

"But my uncle fears snow is coming," Mr. Lefroy said. "If so, even the consolation of hunting will be lost to me."

"So you see, Jane, you've come home just in time! If you had delayed a few days, my nephew might have expired from the tedium of spending all his time with his relations." There was a mischievous sparkle in Madame's fine eyes.

"I say, Aunt, that's not fair," he said, without rancor.

"Ireland!" Jane said without thinking. Madame and her nephew stared. "I beg your pardon, but I was trying to place your accent. Irish, is it not?"

"Yes." Mr. Lefroy was content once more with a monosyllabic answer.

"Tom's father is retired from the army and lives in Limerick, Ireland." Madame hurried to fill the silence. "Tom went to school in Dublin."

"London is a change of scene, to be sure," Jane said. "Do you enjoy your studies?"

"I had better, hadn't I?" he asked, rudely enough to startle her. "It's to be my profession."

Jane stared at him thoughtfully. Amongst the young men of her acquaintance, she found that the younger sons rarely enjoyed the professions decreed for them by wealthier relations. Her brothers had been fortunate that their father had believed that each of them should follow their inclination. She wondered what Tom Lefroy really wanted to do.

The object of her speculation stood up and began pacing about the room. He stopped to examine a drawing on the wall, one of Cassandra's portraits of her sister. He glanced from the drawing to the subject, but did not comment.

Madame's gaze met Jane's, as much as to say, "Did I not tell you?"

Jane answered with an amused smile. She couldn't help it; Mr. Lefroy's manners were unintentionally very humorous. Bedeviling this young man might prove enjoyable.

"Jane, will you be going to the ball tomorrow?" Madame asked.

"There's a ball?" Jane asked.

"A ball? Aunt, you have been withholding vital intelligence," Mr. Lefroy said.

"Nothing too grand," Madame Lefroy said. "The local families pay a subscription and the balls are held in the Basingstoke Assembly Rooms."

"A *public* ball," he said, not bothering to hide his disappointment. "Anyone might come."

"Even yourself," Jane said sweetly. "But do not be afraid. The local inhabitants hardly ever bite strangers."

Hurrying to counteract Jane's impudence, Mrs. Austen said, "The Assembly Balls are always great fun, and one needn't fuss too much about one's wardrobe. In the excitement of your arrival, Jane, I forgot to mention it."

"Of course we will go," Jane said. "Eliza is not too proud to enjoy a country dance, and neither am I." She tossed the words at Mr. Lefroy like a gauntlet. Would he accept the challenge?

Madame said, "Well, Tom, shall we make a party of it? Or are you too superior for such mean entertainment?" He had the grace to look abashed and muttered something to the effect that he knew very few people.

"You have been introduced to us," Jane pointed out. "Have you met my brother James Austen yet?"

"Was he the clergyman from Overton, Aunt?" he said over his shoulder.

"Yes, Tom. We did have the honor of seeing Mr. Austen at the shoot this morning."

"You went too, Madame Lefroy?" Mrs. Austen asked. "I couldn't bear the noise myself."

"When one has a guest, one makes every effort," Madame answered. "Of course, Lucy wanted to come, too. I think she is quite enamored of her cousin." Her tone indicated clearly she thought her daughter's feelings were foolish.

"She's only fifteen," Jane replied, playing up to her friend. "She's far too young to be a sophisticated judge of character. Stranded here in the deadly tedium of the country, she has little opportunity to appreciate a true gentleman."

Tom Lefroy turned to stare at Jane, as if he were truly seeing her for the first time. His eyes were an unusual light green. She had to own he was a handsome young man, with a pale complexion and a fine head of blond hair. His mouth was too small, but his intelligent countenance made up for that . . . or it would if he weren't so disagreeable.

"Miss Austen," he said, continuing to stroll slowly about the room, "you seem determined to pique my interest."

Jane felt herself coloring. He wandered behind the settee where Jane and Madame sat. She deliberately did not look at him. He went on in a condescending drawl, "My aunt said your stories were charming and that I must prevail upon you to read one to me."

"Your aunt is much too kind," Jane said. "I wouldn't dream of inflicting my little scribbles upon you."

"Too bad; I'm sure I could have helped you improve them," he said. "My education has surely been superior to that of any young lady's, no matter how accomplished."

Mrs. Austen said loyally, "Jane's stories are quite good."

"I agree," Madame Lefroy said warmly. "I look forward to seeing them in print."

"Perish the thought," Mrs. Austen said. "No daughter of mine would ever do such a thing. It wouldn't be seemly."

"Is this one of your stories?" Mr. Lefroy asked. Jane twisted her neck to see him holding her latest story up to the light. "You have an uncommonly neat hand," he said, admiring her penmanship.

"Tom!" Madame was furious. To Jane she mouthed the words, "I am sorry."

Trembling with indignation, Jane forced her voice to remain even. "Those papers are mine. I'll thank you not to disturb them." Something in her face must have persuaded him that on this matter she was not to be trifled with, because he quickly replaced them on the desk. Jane leapt to her feet and locked the precious papers away in a drawer. Mr. Lefroy's face didn't express any guilt or shame, but rather sly pleasure.

This Tom Lefroy was not like most young men she knew. Her brothers and their friends might be vulgar, but their manners were always gentlemanly. Even though Jane knew he meant to provoke her, to her great irritation she found she desired his admiration. To impress such a gentleman, against his will as it were, would be a triumph. And it would be a favor to Madame Lefroy besides.

Jane went to the window and turned her back to Mr. Lefroy while she considered how best to manage him.

The drawing room looked out on the garden. Normally a pleasing prospect, most found the view in wintertime bleak without snow to cover the muddy ground. The gardens were brown and dead, and the weather vane in the center of the yard creaked in the wind. A hill full of evergreens rose behind the house.

As Jane stared out of the window, a movement on the hill attracted her eye. Expecting it to be a deer or possibly one of her father's parishioners, she watched carefully. After a moment, she saw the motion again.

Then she caught a glimpse of a scarlet scarf.

CHAPTER 8

*He who, she had been persuaded, would avoid her
as his greatest enemy, seemed, on this accidental
meeting, most eager to preserve the acquaintance.*
PRIDE AND PREJUDICE

𝒟isregarding her mother's protests, Jane wrapped her warmest shawl about her shoulders and hurried out the door. The large garden sloped up to a steep hill studded with fir trees. She took the shortest way to the path, climbing and slipping on the icy ground as she did with barely a moment's thought of her petticoats. Once, she stumbled and fell, breaking her fall with her hands. She clambered to her feet, wiping the dirt from her palms.

She arrived at the spot where she thought the flash of scarlet had originated. She looked down to the parsonage below—yes, this was the spot. But her gentleman-bandit, if bandit he was, had disappeared. She studied the ground but saw neither a footprint nor a conveniently dropped clue to guide her.

Vexed with disappointment, she tightened her woolen wrap about her and turned to retrace her steps back to the house.

"Mademoiselle Austen."

Jane turned slowly to see him standing behind a clump of fir trees. He no longer wore his distinctive hat, but his nose and mouth were covered by his scarf. She could only make out his tawny eyes, staring at her intently.

Jane blushed to realize that he had been watching her. "I do not believe we have been introduced," she said, finding her voice.

"Alas, formal introductions must wait," he said with a quick bow. "I am relieved to see that you reached your destination safely."

"Except for the incident when you shot a gun at my carriage, the journey was uneventful," she said.

"I apologized for that," he protested.

"Did you follow us here?" she asked.

"That is not important," he said. "I must see the Comtesse." From the yearning in his voice, Jane could sense that he longed to see Eliza above all. Jane was in no danger from him.

"Tell me where you are to be found and we shall call on you this afternoon," Jane suggested.

"That is not possible," he said hurriedly. "It is dangerous for me even to be here, hidden among your trees."

"Monsieur, this is ridiculous. Just come to the parsonage and speak with Eliza!"

"Je ne peux pas," he cried, as though his mental state could not be described in English. "I truly cannot. But I hoped to attract your attention so that you could help me. Will you give her something for me, s'il vous plaît?" He drew back his cloak.

Jane tensed, for a wild moment fearing that she had completely misjudged him and he would draw his pistol. But instead he reached into his vest pocket and pulled out a note.

"Step out into the light and I shall consider your request," she countered.

"Mademoiselle, I swear on my honor as a gentleman, I will not harm you or the Comtesse, but you must not see my face."

"Is that because you and I have met before?"

He was silent for a long moment before he said, "Please give this to her immediately."

"Am I to know what it says?" she asked.

"C'est privé," he said.

"Private? How do you know I won't read it?" Jane asked.

"I trust that you will not read a communication meant for someone else. However, I also know the curiosity of an intelligent young woman, and I have no wish for you to compromise your principles. I shall tell you this much: In my note I ask the Comtesse to meet me at the Assembly Ball. It is a public place; she will be perfectly safe."

Jane felt her eyes widen; the stranger was remarkably well informed.

He pressed the note into her hand. Entreating her with his gold-flecked eyes, he said, "S'il vous plaît, mademoiselle?"

Jane eyed the note, observing that the wax seal had no crest pressed into it. An anonymous communication from a stranger—what could be more intriguing? She had to remind herself this was not the time to be imagining possible scenes in a story. After all, what harm could come of giving Eliza a note? Jane was perfectly capable of keeping a watchful eye on her cousin.

"I shall do it," she said.

"Merci! A thousand times, thank you," he said, making that odd gesture of touching his forehead and then his lips that she remembered from their first meeting. Suddenly his gaze traveled beyond their clearing to the parsonage. He tensed. "You have a visitor."

Jane glanced down. A horse was galloping up the lane leading to the house. The rider was cloaked and wore a regimental hat. Not until he dismounted and swept off his hat did Jane recognize her brother. "Henry!" she called.

Henry's head jerked, and his eyes searched the gardens. She called again. Finally he spied her. "Jane, come down!" he called.

She turned to say farewell, but the mysterious gentleman had disappeared amongst the firs. She tucked his note into the pocket she wore under her skirt. Then she half ran, half fell down the hill to Henry. He caught her when she stumbled at the bottom.

"Jane! What are you doing out in this weather?" He glanced toward the ridge where she had been standing.

"I was communing with my muse," she confided with a smile. Henry was the brother who most admired her writing.

"Your stories aren't worth freezing for," Henry said, laughing.

"What are you doing here?" she asked as she hugged him tightly.

"Your hands are freezing! Let's get you inside," he said.

At six feet and fair with brilliant hazel eyes, Henry was the handsomest of the Austen sons. He was also Jane's favorite of all her brothers; he was the most amusing and the one who understood her best. Beneath his dark cloak she could see his bright red officer's coat. Henry had tried being a clergyman, but found the busy social life in the military more to his taste. He was stationed in Southampton and Jane had not seen him in several months.

"Aren't you needed with your regiment?" she asked.

"I have a few days' leave and I heard you were home," he said. "And Eliza, too. How could I stay away? If only Cassandra had come, my happiness would be complete."

Jane stepped back, eyeing her brother. Since her decision to come home had been made only a day or so ago, she wondered exactly how he had heard the news. No sooner had she posed the question to herself than her own reasoning gave her the answer. "Edward sent you!" she cried.

Henry took a half step back. He opened his mouth, ready with a glib denial, but then his laughing eyes met hers. "I never could deceive you. Yes, Edward suggested I come. And somehow our dear brother has the ear of my commanding officer."

"You're here to spy on Eliza for the War Office!" she accused, jabbing her finger in his chest.

All injured innocence, he rubbed where she had poked him. "Not to spy. I'm here to protect her from being bothered." He grinned. "And it's no hardship, I assure you. This is the perfect opportunity to press my suit with her."

"You always did admire her," Jane said, shaking her head. "But, Henry, she is out of your reach."

Henry's face took on an offended air. "Why? I have good prospects, don't I?"

Jane shrugged.

"Am I not considered handsome?"

"Of course!" She laughed.

"Well, then! Eliza is unencumbered by a husband, and I'm willing to volunteer to make up the lack."

"Her husband has been dead for only a year—and she's ten years your elder!" Jane pointed out.

"She is fourteen years older than you, yet you are close friends," Henry retorted.

"Have you forgotten she has a son?" Jane continued.

"Hastings likes me. I adore Eliza. She has a fortune, which is very welcome. And she's part of the family. It's perfect."

"I still don't think much of your chances," Jane said. "A wealthy widow can do better than one of her poor Austen cousins, no matter how charming."

Henry was not offended. Like Eliza, he rarely took anything seriously. Jane reconsidered; the two might indeed make a good match.

"Besides, you might have competition if Mother has anything to say about it," Jane added mischievously.

Henry's eyes narrowed. "What do you mean?"

"Mother sees *James* as Eliza's perfect husband and she his second wife. He could settle her flighty ways, Mother thinks. Can't you see Eliza as a clergyman's wife?"

Henry burst out laughing. "Your teasing will be the death of me. As if Eliza could prefer stick-in-the-mud James to me!" He took her arm. "Come in the house before you freeze. Whatever were you doing outside?"

Before she could answer, they were in the parlor. Madame Lefroy was delighted to see Henry, and Mrs. Austen even found enough energy to stand to greet her son. Mr. Tom Lefroy professed himself pleased to make Henry's acquaintance. Eliza, downstairs at last, greeted Henry warmly. To Jane's watchful gaze, Eliza seemed to find Henry entirely satisfactory. Henry, in his turn, was ardent in his admiration of Eliza's new hairstyle.

Stepping away from the hubbub, Jane thought about the note in her pocket. She wished she wasn't too honorable to read it. She knew that if Henry or Edward had charge of the note that they would convince themselves it was in Eliza's best interest for them to do so. Which was why Jane had undertaken to protect Eliza herself.

As Henry paid his compliments to his mother and Madame Lefroy, Jane felt a prickling on the back of her neck. She turned her head slightly to see Tom Lefroy watching her. He stood in the corner alone, a book in his hand. Once he caught her eye, his gaze went deliberately to the window and up the hill outside, then back to Jane.

She deliberately made her face blank; it was none of Mr. Lefroy's business what she had been doing on the hill. Without thinking, she checked that her hair had not been loosened by her exertions outside.

Mr. Lefroy bowed mockingly.

Mortified that he thought she was preening for him, she moved to take a seat next to Eliza.

"Good morning, Jane," Eliza said. "Or gracious, I suppose I should say good afternoon."

"I hope you slept well," Jane said.

"Of course. When I am at Steventon, I am at home," Eliza said simply. "But what have you been doing? Your mother has been beside herself." Her eyes lit on the mud still falling in lumps from Jane's skirts. "From the state of your petticoats, I suspect you went outside despite the chill."

"My petticoats are often the despair of any woman with a sense of style," Jane agreed with a rueful smile.

"Happily you have many other excellent qualities," Eliza said generously. "Don't you agree, Mr. Lefroy?" she called to Mr. Lefroy standing a few feet away.

Mr. Lefroy was absorbed in his book. Jane strained to read the title. She blushed when she saw it was *Tom Jones*, a novel that, despite its age, still scandalized the gentry.

"I beg your pardon?" he asked.

"I said that my cousin, Miss Austen, is very accomplished. Her stories are very amusing, and she plays the pianoforte very well. She is the finest embroiderer in the family, and her penmanship is so precise as to be the equal of any printer's type."

"Eliza, stop!" Jane hissed.

"Madame Lefroy has acquainted me with her plan regarding Mr. Lefroy," Eliza whispered behind her hand. "I cannot resist helping a little."

"Perhaps you should administer the lesson yourself?" Jane suggested.

"He's too young for me," Eliza said. She raised her voice for Mr. Lefroy's benefit. "And tomorrow you will have the pleasure of seeing Miss Austen dance. There are few things prettier to watch."

"A woman's figure does appear to the greatest advantage when she is moving," Mr. Lefroy agreed, placing a piece of ribbon to mark his page. He approached the two ladies. "For instance, Miss Austen was quite graceful when she suddenly left to climb the hill behind this house to meet someone in the woods."

"Jane! How unaccountable," Eliza said. "You must tell me everything!"

"I agree; please tell us everything," Mr. Lefroy said, watching Jane closely.

"Mr. Lefroy, you are making a trivial matter seem quite mysterious," Jane answered. The last thing she needed was Mr. Lefroy prying into her and Eliza's private affairs. "I briefly excused myself because I thought I saw a tramp in the woods. I've heard about a man trespassing in our firs."

"All the more reason to stay indoors," Eliza exclaimed.

"Miss Austen, what exactly would you have done if you had found him? Weren't you afraid?" Mr. Lefroy asked. She noticed that his habitual pose of leaning away had been abandoned. He was interested now in spite of himself.

"Steventon is perfectly safe, Mr. Lefroy. As you yourself have noted, nothing ever happens here," Jane said. "And as it happened, I was mistaken. There was no one there. But if there had been, I would have offered him a hot meal and a spot in our barn. It's too cold for anyone to sleep out of doors."

Eliza beamed. "That's very kind, Jane."

"I daresay I must add charity to your list of accomplishments," Mr. Lefroy said.

Jane's color rose at his mocking tone. She resented his assumption that he, as an eligible gentleman, had the right to judge her accomplishments—or lack of them.

"For shame, Mr. Lefroy," Eliza said indignantly. "I assure you that Jane, nay, her entire family, is always charitable. Quite remarkably so when you consider their modest fortune. I, on the other hand, do not possess a generous bone in my body."

Henry took this opportunity to hurry to Eliza's side and contradict her. "Nonsense, Eliza, you are generosity itself."

"When it suits me," Eliza admitted, looking up at Henry through her long eyelashes. "But I believe that Jane gets real pleasure in helping people, even when it is inconvenient."

The conversation moved on to other topics and became general. Jane spoke little. How much had Mr. Lefroy seen from the window? When her attention returned to the group, they were discussing the Assembly Ball. Madame Lefroy was content to sit to one side, watching with a resigned smile.

Eliza held court in the center of the room. "It's been many years since I went to a ball that required a paid subscription," she said. "The last time I went to one was before my marriage," she added in a reminiscing tone.

Mr. Lefroy looked puzzled. "Oh, will your husband be joining us, Madame?"

There was an awkward silence, broken by the always tactful Madame Lefroy. "The Comtesse is a widow, Tom. She is only just out of mourning."

"I . . . beg your pardon," he stammered. "I wasn't aware."

Jane found herself mildly satisfied at his embarrassment and then scolded herself for such ill nature.

"Nonsense," Eliza assured him. "How were you to know?"

Prudence's arrival with tea further relieved the embarrassment in the room. Unlike in London, an afternoon visit in the country was likely to last for several hours. Jane had whiled away many a day at Madame Lefroy's home, reading in her extensive library. However, Tom Lefroy seemed unaware of his social obligations and, as soon as his empty teacup was replaced loudly in its saucer, he began to pace about the room, glancing frequently at the clock. Finally, Mrs. Austen suggested that they play a hand of whist. Henry immediately claimed Eliza as his partner, but she refused, saying laughingly, "I do not have a head for cards."

Jane saw her opportunity to speak quietly with Eliza. She said, "Henry, you partner Madame Lefroy and Mr. Lefroy shall partner Mother."

Mr. Lefroy's face fell. Madame Lefroy hid a smile behind her fan.

Soon the others were playing cards at a table near the window, leaving Eliza and Jane by the fire. Making sure she was not overheard, Jane told Eliza about her encounter in the woods.

"I *knew* something had happened," Eliza exclaimed. "But I think you were terribly reckless."

Jane shrugged. "He has no interest in hurting me. He wants to see you."

"Then why doesn't he just come to the door and knock?" Eliza asked peevishly.

"I don't know," Jane said. "He wants to talk to you at the ball. He gave me a note with the particulars."

"He will be at the ball?" Eliza clapped her hands with delight, drawing Henry's attention from the card table. Mrs. Austen rapped him on the arm with her fan, calling him back to the game.

"Lower your voice," Jane cautioned.

"Now I shall have something to look forward to tomorrow night," Eliza went on. "What else does the note say?"

"I didn't read it," Jane said virtuously.

"Why not? I would have," Eliza said. She held out her hand. "Give it to me, s'il te plaît."

Eliza broke the seal, dropping bits of red wax onto the carpet. She unfolded the note. Jane could see it was written in a bold hand on heavy, expensive paper . She thought she could spot a few words of French.

Eliza gasped, and the blood drained from her face.

"Eliza, what is it?" Jane whispered.

The note fell from Eliza's trembling hand.

"What does it say to affect you so?" Jane asked, leaning down to retrieve the letter.

"Don't read that! Give it to me!" Eliza said loudly. The card players looked over. Mr. Lefroy was as alert as a fox-hound that has caught the scent.

Jane handed the letter to Eliza, but before she could say a word, Eliza had ripped the note into two pieces and tossed the paper in the fire. She stood up and left the room.

Jane watched the paper catch fire and burn to ash. For an instant, the ink outlasted the paper and the signatory line was legible—a bold initial *J*.

CHAPTER 9

It was moonlight, and every body
was full of engagements.
SENSE AND SENSIBILITY

*J*ane sat down at her writing desk. Taking up her pen,
she wrote:

> *Dear Cassandra,*
> *The moon is full and the local gentry are dreadfully bored so I*
> *expect everyone, with the distressing exception of you, will be at the*
> *Basingstoke Assembly Ball tonight. Even Mr. Tom Lefroy may*
> *deign to come. Did I tell you about him when I wrote yesterday? I*
> *hold him of so little account that I might have neglected to mention*

him in my last letter. After all, what is a young law student in comparison to a pistol-wielding highwayman?

Mr. Lefroy is Madame's nephew and about one and twenty years of age. His countenance is handsome; or, rather, it would be if he weren't always sneering at his unlucky companions. Madame has intimated that she would be delighted if I put him in his place, and if my mind is not too occupied with Eliza's intrigues, I may just do it. He is a young man whose manners need humbling.

Eliza, as you know, is always elegant, but this afternoon she has prepared her toilette with surprising special care. You will be glad to know that Eliza's new short hair has not prevented her from curling what is left most becomingly and adorning it with a bandeau of pearls. Her dress is a pale yellow silk, with a bodice cut daringly low—such is the latest fashion. I laughed and reminded her that it is only a country ball. But she waved away my remonstrations.

We still have an hour before her carriage is to take us to the ball. In the meantime, Eliza is trying to teach poor James to dance. She teases him that he must find a new wife. Our earnest brother flushes crimson and stammers but cannot bring himself to express his admiration for her.

Upstairs I hear Henry shouting for his boot polish. Henry is so dashing in his uniform; I greatly fear that he will thoroughly overshadow our older brother and establish himself as Eliza's favorite. Who among us can resist a red coat? Not Eliza!

As I watch her teaching James the steps of a Boulanger, she laughs gaily but I sense she is distracted. As I told you in my letter yesterday, "J" is waiting for her at the ball. Naturally I do not intend to let her meet him alone, but I greatly fear that she will try to do just that. So instead of anticipating a night of lively dancing, I shall be chaperoning my cousin, a lady of greater years and infinitely more experience. I wish, dear Cassandra, that you were here to help.

I shall finish this letter after the ball.

Jane blotted her letter and slipped it inside her writing desk. She stood up and went to the mirror to check her hair-dressing.

"Jane!" Eliza called impatiently from the center of the parlor. "Surely you aren't wearing *that* to the ball!"

Glancing down at her simple white muslin, a dress that had already seen several seasons, Jane shrugged. "What am I to do? This quarter's dress allowance is long spent."

"But the waistline is too low," Eliza cried. "It should come up to here." She lifted her hands underneath her bosom. Jane couldn't help but notice the narrow band of fabric between the high waist and Eliza's low bodice. "An empire waistline is most flattering to a fine figure like yours," she said. She circled Jane reprovingly. "And there's no train!"

"That particular fashion hasn't reached Hampshire yet," Jane said, laughing. "But I did read about it in *The Lady's Magazine*."

"Aha! You pretend to be so literary, but I knew you secretly read the fashion papers! In London, a lady cannot be seen without a long tail," Eliza insisted. She unhooked her dress and let the train flare on the floor around her feet. Jane caught her breath at the easy elegance of it. What she wouldn't give for a dress like that! Jane promised herself if she ever wrote a rich heroine in one of her stories, this would be exactly the dress she would wear.

"So you just hook it back up when you want to move around," James said in a bid to win back Eliza's attention. "That's very ingenious, Eliza. I am always astounded by how clever women are with their clothes."

"Dear James, you must never compliment a lady on her dress," Eliza scolded.

"Why not?" he asked.

"You may take it for granted that we shall be dressed suitably," Jane said.

"Then how am I to express my admiration?" he asked.

"You may flatter her lively dancing. Or her complexion. Or her fine eyes. That is perfectly acceptable," Eliza added.

James was darker than Henry, with bushy eyebrows that he now drew together in a glower. "How is a fellow to know what to say?" he asked plaintively.

"I shall help you," Eliza promised. "But first we must take care of Jane. She can't possibly find a husband wearing that!"

"Eliza, this is my best dress," Jane said lightly, although in her heart she longed for a dress that hadn't been reworked for three seasons running. "Besides, I am not looking for a husband."

"Nonsense," Eliza said. "Why else go to the ball?"

Jane was silent. Eliza's words had the ring of truth. Every ball was a matrimonial opportunity. Just because she hated it didn't make it false.

"You may borrow a dress of mine," Eliza insisted. She went to the stairs and called for Marie. "You must look your best if you are to dance with the dashing Mr. Lefroy."

"That's hardly likely," Jane said, although she suspected he might dance rather well.

"Jane, he knows no one else. Of course he'll ask you to dance."

"So if only he knew more people I wouldn't have to suffer his attentions," Jane said mockingly.

Marie appeared, flushed from running. She was wearing a cast-off gown of Eliza's. Jane stifled a pang of envy that Eliza's maid was more fashionable than Jane herself.

After Eliza gave her maid instructions, Jane followed Marie out of the room, wondering whether her cousin's motives were purely altruistic. Perhaps Eliza wanted to ensure that Jane was fully occupied for the entire evening to distract her from a clandestine rendezvous.

As she reached the second floor landing, she heard James telling Eliza her cheeks were shining with the exertions of her dancing. Jane spared a moment to hope that James's heart would not be too badly bruised.

Eliza's room was unrecognizable from the days when Jane's brothers stayed there. It was filled with trunks, and dresses, scarves, and shawls were scattered across every surface. Jane thought Eliza must be exhausting to dress. Marie's lovely dark eyes looked tired, and Jane felt guilty for making more work for the maid.

While Marie looked through the clothes, Jane wandered about the room. Next to Eliza's bed was a framed double portrait she had never seen before. She picked it up. On the right side was a miniature of Eliza's dead husband, Jean. He was handsome, though more in a French style than English. His nose was long and aristocratic and his bright eyes seemed to know her deepest desires. Jane didn't wonder that Eliza's heart had been ensnared by him. On the opposite side, the painter had depicted Eliza's son, Hastings.

"That is an attractive portrait," Jane said.

"Yes. Madame does not travel anywhere without it," Marie said, pulling from a trunk a white muslin trimmed with a delicate lace around the bodice. "Madame suggested this dress."

Jane couldn't take her eyes from the gown, so well cut and fashionable.

Marie continued, "The queen made this classical style very popular a few years ago." Jane realized that when Marie said the queen she meant Marie Antoinette, not England's Queen Charlotte. Naturally, Eliza's servants would be royalists.

At Marie's signal, Jane lifted her arms and Marie expertly removed her dress and slipped on the new one. "As you see, it is very flattering to your height. En fait, it is more suitable for a girl your age than the Comtesse."

Jane, admiring the dress in the long mirror, lifted her eyebrows. Marie didn't meet her gaze but busied herself pulling the bodice's drawstring tighter. Jane nervously watched her bosom in the mirror, but Marie knew her craft and Jane's decorum stayed intact.

Marie's ministrations had pulled a thread loose, and she drew a pair of long-bladed scissors from a custom pocket tied around her waist and snipped it off. Jane stared down at the sharp blades. "Those are handsome scissors."

"Oui," Marie said. "I always travel with my own tools."

"Do you do all of Madame's sewing?"

"Bien sûr. Since Madame lost her husband I have had to take in all her gowns; she has lost so much weight." She eyed Jane critically. "Your topaz necklace is very nice with that neckline, but you need earrings." She rummaged in Eliza's jewelry box and found a pair of teardrop earrings in the same stone. "Yes. These will do nicely."

Jane obediently put them on, feeling rather daring. She was not in the habit of wearing jewelry, mostly because she owned so few pieces. "What about my hair?" she ventured to ask.

Marie stepped back and examined her subject. "You have beautiful hair. We call it *marron*, the word in English is chestnut, I believe? The latest fashion is to sweep it up and leave it loose—but I am certain you are a lively dancer and we must plan accordingly." She unpinned Jane's shoulder-length hair and began to brush it with slow strokes.

"Not too lively a dancer, I hope?" Jane asked with embarrassment.

"Of course not, mademoiselle is a perfect lady." With deft hands, Marie arranged Jane's hair into a style that looked very natural, but was cleverly pinned to stay in place. Jane's hair was naturally curly, and Marie left the ringlets to adorn her face.

"Voilà," Marie said, stepping back and inviting Jane to examine her reflection.

Jane thought she looked rather well. "Don't get any ideas, Miss Jane Austen," she reminded herself. "At the end of the day you still have no fortune and no prospects."

"What did you say, mademoiselle?" Marie asked.

"Nothing." She paused. "Merci," she said gratefully.

As Jane watched Marie make her final adjustments to the gown she noticed two gold chains swinging from the girl's neck. From one dangled a cross and from the other an expensive locket of finely worked gold. Jane would have been delighted to own either, and she wondered that a servant had such jewelry.

"That is a lovely locket," Jane said.

Marie straightened up, throwing her shoulders back. "Ah, merci. It was a gift from my employer."

Jane nodded. So this was how Eliza won the hearts of her servants—she bribed them with fancy gifts. "May I see it?" she asked.

Slowly, Marie took off the necklace and handed it to Jane.

When Jane opened it, she was surprised to see a little boy, about the same age as Hastings. But this boy looked alert and curious. His dark eyes almost shone. "A handsome lad," Jane said.

"My son, Daniel," Marie said proudly.

Jane was taken aback. How singular of Eliza to keep a maid who had a child. A lady's maid was supposed to be unmarried and certainly not a mother. "Where is he now?" she asked curiously.

"In London, at Madame's house. She is very kind. She helped me bring him here from France, and she allows the boy to stay in the house."

"He must be of an age with Hastings."

"Daniel is younger, mais . . ." Marie gave Jane a knowing look. Hastings might be the son of the Comte, but he would never be healthy enough or strong enough to be the head of the household, assuming the French Republic ever returned the Comte's estate to his heir. "Poor Madame."

"It is tragic," Jane agreed. She knew exactly how Eliza felt. She had an older brother who the family never mentioned. George was subject to fits and was unable to speak or hear. Long ago Mrs. Austen had sent the boy to live with a local family in nearby Deane. Tomorrow, if the weather remained fine, Jane would visit him.

"He looks like you," Jane said.

"No," Marie said flatly. "He resembles his father."

Jane recalled Eliza telling her that Marie's husband had been killed in France. "You must miss him," Jane said with sympathy, not sure whether she meant Daniel or René.

"Naturellement." The finality in her tone warned Jane not to say anything else.

Prudence came to the door. "Miss Austen! The carriage is here." She made a face at Marie's back, and Jane had to duck her head to hide her amusement. Eliza might have endeared herself to the servants, but her maid was not as popular. Of course, Prudence was a country girl who distrusted "Frenchies" on principle. It was beyond her to make a distinction between the French revolutionaries who threatened to invade England and the émigrés who had fled the Reign of Terror to find sanctuary.

"Attendez, mademoiselle, you cannot go without gloves," Marie said, pulling out a long pair of white gloves made of kid leather.

Jane looked at her own cloth gloves. "What is wrong with mine?" she asked, although she realized as she spoke that it was evident where they had been darned more than once.

"Madame would insist," Marie said firmly.

Finally, dressed and feeling like royalty herself, Jane made her way downstairs. Her mother, in a quilted dressing gown and mobcap, was waiting to see them off. "I am sorry indeed that I cannot come tonight," she said. "But my nerves won't stand for a noisy party."

"Mrs. Austen, you must rest," Eliza said kindly. "I shall look after Jane."

Jane lifted her eyebrows, knowing the opposite was more likely.

"See that you do!" Mrs. Austen said. "She is wont to choose cleverness over propriety."

"Mother, I'm nineteen and can look after myself," Jane replied. "Besides, it's a Basingstoke Assembly Ball. I already know every gentleman who will be there; no one will require an introduction to dance with me."

"Nevertheless," Mrs. Austen said, "behave yourself."

"She will," Henry promised, resplendent in white breeches and bright red coat. "I'll make sure of it. Especially when she looks so well tonight." He smiled appreciatively at Jane, and then bowed to Eliza, showing he knew perfectly well who was responsible for Jane's good looks this evening.

James, practical and dull in dark coat and black breeches, glanced at his sister and said, "You look different. Did you change your hair?"

"Cousin James," Eliza said, hitting him gently on the arm with her fan. "You are impossible. I don't know what to do with you!"

James seemed to gather his nerve. "Eliza, I insist you reserve the first two dances for myself."

Jane and her mother exchanged anxious looks. Eliza, even as a widowed countess, was likely to be the highest ranked at the ball, so it would fall to her and her partner to open the first dance, and all eyes would be watching. James couldn't possibly dance well enough to withstand such scrutiny.

"Cousin James," Eliza said after the briefest pause. "If only you had asked me earlier. Henry has already claimed the first two dances."

Henry's startled expression was swiftly replaced by a complacent one. "Too bad, brother!" he said cheerfully.

James's face was thunderous but Eliza appeased him by patting him on the arm and promising him the supper dance, which gave him the honor of taking her into supper and sitting with her there.

Before the silence could become more awkward, Jacques appeared at the front door. A blast of wind made Jane wish she had a warmer shawl.

Inclining his head to Eliza, he said, "Madame, the coach is ready."

James, his face still sulky, went first to hold the door. Next to his younger brother, Jane couldn't help comparing them to a drab wren and a flamboyant peacock. Both were excellent birds with many worthy qualities, but the latter would always attract more notice.

Henry proffered his arm to Eliza, and with a flirtatious smile, she tucked her hand in his elbow. Jane gave James her hand, murmuring, "Darling brother, Eliza's like a magpie, attracted to the bright and shiny. Do you really think she is the wife for a solemn clergyman?"

His eyes met hers, and she was saddened to see the hurt there. "I'd have a chance if it weren't for Henry."

"And every other officer at the ball," Jane pointed out. "Eliza's preference will always be for the lighthearted over the respectable." James shook his head, and Jane knew she was wasting her breath.

Jacques had placed foot warmers on the floor of the carriage and draped two fur rugs over the seat. Eliza and Jane huddled under the rugs. Eliza seemed distracted, and

Jane wondered if she were worried about meeting the mysterious *J.*

To distract her, Jane asked, "What will you choose for the first dance?"

Eliza's full attention was engaged now. "Are you certain I will be the one to call it?"

"Almost definitely. I can't think of anyone who might come who could compete with your rank."

"Perhaps the minuet?" Eliza suggested with a smile.

Henry groaned. "Not that old dance—it's devilishly complicated."

"And French!" James said. "I mean no offense, Eliza, but it would be in poor taste while we're at war."

"We're to give up a dance because of the war?" Eliza pouted. "Does that mean we should renounce French wines? Or cheeses? Or silk stockings?"

Since all those things were indeed banned, Jane didn't respond.

"With whom shall you dance tonight?" Eliza asked Jane.

Jane shrugged. "The usual gentlemen, I suppose. There is remarkably little variety at a Basingstoke Assembly."

"What about Mr. Lefroy?"

"If he deigns to come, I am certain he will be too discourteous to dance, no matter how many women require partners."

"Lefroy seemed like a decent chap to me," Henry said.

"Then you must not have spoken with him for any length of time," Jane retorted. Eliza and Henry exchanged amused glances.

The eight-mile drive to Basingstoke passed remarkably quickly. Henry commented that the frozen road made for a fast trip. Jane stared out the window at the farms and fields, brightly illuminated by the full moon. She loved driving at night but since the Austens couldn't afford to keep their own carriage, she rarely had the opportunity.

They pulled into the Market Place, a large square filled with small shops and dominated at one end by the Angel Inn. The inn was built above a courtyard, allowing carriages to enter beneath it. The road and courtyard were lined with torches, and at the back of the courtyard Jane glimpsed the windows of the ballroom glowing from the candlelit chandeliers inside. This was always her favorite moment of coming to a ball. It was a scene from fantasia: the excited voices, the women in their finery, the flickering firelight and smoke. For a fleeting moment, it felt as if anything might happen.

Finally, it was their turn to disembark. Henry took Eliza's hand and helped her down. Before James remembered to do the same for her, Jane hopped out, following Eliza through the inn door and then up the flight of stairs leading to the Assembly Rooms.

At the top, she noticed a fine figure of a man outlined in the golden candlelight coming from the ballroom. He waited at the landing, as if he were waiting for her. Who could it be? Her heart beat a little faster. She touched her borrowed earrings and smoothed a curl on her neck.

The man turned to see her coming up the stairs. "Miss Austen." He bowed. "How delightful to see you again. I've been looking forward to continuing our conversation."

She sighed. It was only Tom Lefroy.

CHAPTER 10

To be fond of dancing was a certain
step towards falling in love.
PRIDE AND PREJUDICE

"*M*ister Lefroy," Jane said, with the barest suggestion of a curtsy. Naturally he would be the first person she saw at the ball.

"May I help you with your coat?" he asked, intercepting a servant who was waiting to collect her wrap. A few feet away, Henry helped Eliza off with her fur-lined pelisse; Eliza's blush told Jane that his attentions were not unwelcome. James tossed his greatcoat to a servant and strode toward the ballroom without a word.

"I am perfectly capable of taking off my own coat, Mr. Lefroy," Jane answered.

"Jane!" Eliza whispered. "What would your mother say?"

"Very well, Miss Austen," Mr. Lefroy said, stepping back.

Jane fumbled with the hooks at her neck, her hands suddenly clumsy. Her face felt warm, and Eliza's amusement made it worse.

"Perhaps I may be of assistance after all?" he asked.

"Very well," Jane said, embarrassed. As Mr. Lefroy unhooked the pelisse and lifted it from her shoulders, his fingers grazed her neck. Unexpectedly his touch made her shiver. She took a breath to compose herself as Mr. Lefroy handed her coat to a servant. "Thank you," she said.

"Shall we go inside?" Henry said, offering Eliza his arm.

"Yes, shall we?" Mr. Lefroy extended his elbow to Jane. Careful to let her hand rest only lightly on his arm, she accepted.

As they walked down the long corridor lit with ensconced candles, Mr. Lefroy looked about. Jane was preoccupied trying to reconcile her impressions of him. In her parlor he had been insufferable. But tonight he was rather different. Clearly he was making an effort to be pleasant. In fact, she was the one being churlish. She resolved to do better.

"Are we above the coach house then?" he asked. He couldn't quite hide his disdain for a country-dance.

"Yes," Jane answered. Roguishly she added, "And the ballroom is over the stable."

"I see. Horse manure and ladies' perfume," he said with a dismal expression. "How singular. I did not plan to dance anyway."

Jane lifted her eyebrows; perhaps her first impression had been correct after all. Manners might be different in Ireland, but in Hampshire, a single gentleman who did not dance was considered terribly rude. "I am surprised that you honored us with your presence at all."

"My aunt insisted," he said dismissively.

In front of them, Eliza glanced back at Jane; Jane couldn't tell whether Eliza was reevaluating Mr. Lefroy's charms on Jane's behalf or scheming to escape Jane's watchful eye. Oblivious to all the undercurrents around him, Henry knocked on the double doors to the ballroom. A large man with a florid complexion opened the doors.

"Mr. Austen," he bellowed. "And Miss Austen. Welcome to the Assembly Ball."

"Mr. Bigg-Wither," Jane said, wincing at the looks his loud voice attracted. "How do you do?" She curtsyed.

"Very well, very well indeed," he answered. "I am the master of ceremonies tonight, you know." Mr. Bigg-Wither was the largest landowner in the area, and his sense of importance was commensurate with the extent of his property.

"Yes, it is the talk of the county," Jane said. "Congratulations."

Henry interjected, "May we introduce you to our cousin, Madame La Comtesse de Feuillide?"

Mr. Bigg-Wither bowed so low Jane was afraid he would tip over. "Comtesse," he said. "I am delighted to make your acquaintance. I had heard you were favoring the district with your presence."

Beside her, Mr. Lefroy whispered in Jane's ear, "She's a minor countess, not the queen!"

Jane pressed her lips together to keep a giggle from escaping. She tapped his arm sharply with her fan and stepped away from him. Eliza ignored them; no flattery was too unctuous for her so long as she was the subject of it. "Charmed, I am sure," she said.

"We are particularly counting on you to open the ball," Mr. Bigg-Wither said.

"I would be delighted, Mr. Withers-Bigg," she said.

Keeping his face composed, Henry murmured, "Cousin, it is Mr. Biggs-Withers."

"Oh," Eliza said, putting her gloved fingers to her lips. "I beg your pardon, Mr. Biggs-Withers. Mr. Austen shall be my partner for the evening. And Jane must take the second position," Eliza insisted. She looked expectantly at Mr. Lefroy, ignoring the slightest shake of Jane's head.

Mr. Bigg-Wither looked uncomfortable, and not just because of Eliza's inability to say his name. No doubt she had upset his carefully planned arrangements of dancers, but he rose to the occasion. "I have the perfect partner for you, Miss Austen." He beckoned to someone just inside the ballroom out of Jane's line of sight. "I believe you know my eldest son, Harris."

The doorway was all at once filled with the bulk of Harris Bigg-Wither. Jane knew him to be a clumsy oaf. In addition, he was several years Jane's junior. Her heart sank. To dance in the first group for the first dance should be a triumph, but to dance it with Harris would be humiliating.

"M-m-miss Austen," Harris said. "It's a p-p-pleasure to see you."

"Ask her for the first *two* dances," his father whispered, all too audibly.

With a flash of inspiration, Jane said with a curtsy, "Mr. Bigg-Wither, I'm sorry, but I am engaged for the first two dances. Mr. Lefroy has already asked me."

As smoothly as if she had warned him of her stratagem, Mr. Lefroy gave his arm with a decided flourish to Jane. "My apologies, Mr. Bigg-Wither, but you must be quicker if you want to claim such a prize."

Harris mumbled his excuses and fled back to the ballroom. His father looked irritated. "Comtesse," he said, "the dance will begin momentarily." With a sour look at Mr. Lefroy, he scurried inside with a speed surprising in someone his size.

Henry led Eliza into the ballroom, leaving Jane alone with Mr. Lefroy. She pulled her arm out of his grasp. "While I appreciate your help, I do not care for your wording. I'm no man's prize," she said.

Mr. Lefroy regarded her solemnly. "Would you rather dance with the gallant Harris?" he asked.

Jane was conflicted, a condition she found to be unsettling. Finally she admitted, "I'd sooner dance with an ox. My pride may be injured but my toes will stay intact." Then, knowing that common courtesy demanded a least a little effort from her, she added, "Thank you for allowing yourself to be of use in my moment of need."

"What would you have done if I had already been engaged?" he asked mockingly.

"I must say I hadn't considered the possibility," Jane said with a raised brow. She let the words float on the air before softening them. "You said you were not planning to dance. And after all, you know very few young ladies in Hampshire." It may have been her imagination, but color seemed to creep up his neck.

He cleared his throat. "Fortunately for you, I have only just arrived. And perhaps I was too hasty when I said I wouldn't dance. I did not know then that I could aspire to have the indomitable Miss Jane Austen as my partner."

Jane watched him warily, weighing his words for sincerity or sarcasm. Indomitable could be interpreted in several ways.

He continued, "Even if the conclusion is foregone . . . may I have the honor of this dance?"

Jane decided to give in to the situation. She extended her hand, glad for Eliza's elegant kid gloves. "You may indeed, Mr. Lefroy."

He led her into the ballroom and she took a certain satisfaction at the surprise on his face. The room was large and elegant. Fireplaces at either end blazed merrily. There were windows along one side and mirrors on the other, so the room looked even bigger than it was. An enormous chandelier, resplendent with candles, illuminated every corner and was reflected in the polished floor. The forgiving light flattered the complexions of the ladies, young and old.

There was an air of expectancy, heightened by the humming and scraping of the fiddlers as they tuned their instruments. The band consisted of a violin, a three-stringed double bass, flute, English horn, and a piano. Refreshments were prepared in the corner opposite the musicians. The chaperones, mostly mothers and aunts who no longer danced, were already gathered by the fires and happily gossiping. An open door led to the card room. The ballroom was already almost full; it seemed that all the local gentry was in attendance.

"Which dance will your cousin choose?" Mr. Lefroy asked Jane but her answer was lost to the great pounding of Mr. Bigg-Wither's staff as he announced the first dance. The center of the room cleared of everyone except the dancers. Mr. Bigg-Wither quickly arranged a dozen couples, with Henry and Eliza first in the line, facing each other. Mr. Lefroy and Jane were next.

Henry and Eliza made a decidedly handsome couple— she in her fashionable pale yellow gown and he with his red coat, its gold trim glittering in the candlelight.

"The first dance of this Assembly shall be called by our honored guest, the Comtesse de Feuillide!" Mr. Bigg-Wither trumpeted. With a bow in Eliza's direction, he asked, "Madame, what dance shall it be?"

"I believe the Assembly would be best served by a dance to honor our fine men in uniform!" Eliza batted her eyes at Henry. "Let us start with 'The Glorious First of June,' and let it be done in the liveliest manner!"

The dance was a popular one as it celebrated the British Navy's defeat of the French several years before. Henry, along with every officer in the room, looked pleased. Eliza gave Jane a triumphant look, and Jane nodded her approval.

Jane would rather like to see what the War Office would say to that patriotic choice.

As she waited for the music to start, Jane found herself praying for just one thing: to let Mr. Lefroy dance well. It was not so much to ask, was it?

Mr. Lefroy leaned toward her and spoke softly into her ear. "My aunt tells me you are a fine dancer."

"She is very kind," Jane said, blushing. Then she recovered her wits. "And if I asked Madame Lefroy about your dancing, what would she say?"

His eyes playful, he teased, "It's too late to ask now."

There was a swell of cheerful music. Each couple bowed to each other. Then Eliza and Henry moved toward each other, clasping their right hands and turning several times. They exchanged places with Mr. Lefroy and Jane. Another set of turns, this time restoring Eliza and Henry to the first position. Eliza and Henry promenaded down the line of dancers and back up again. Finally Eliza and Henry switched places with Mr. Lefroy and Jane, who began the next set.

To Jane's relief, Mr. Lefroy was an excellent dancer. On the turns he was as nimble and lively as Jane. He knew the trick of pressing his hands against hers so there was tension between their bodies—that was the secret to looking well on the dance floor.

"You're familiar with our country dances, I see," Jane said, exhilarated and breathless as they finished their turn and waited while the other ten couples completed the steps.

"We had dances like this all the time in Limerick," he said. She thought she detected a hint of wistfulness. "The London dances aren't the same."

"I'm sure there are other entertainments to suit you," Jane answered, remembering that Madame Lefroy had said her nephew had fallen in with a disreputable crowd.

"That is precisely what worries my great-uncle." Mr. Lefroy laughed. But his face sobered and his tone grew serious. "And since all my career prospects rest in his hands, I am bound to do as he says."

With a flourish, each of the pairs came back together and everyone took hands to dance in a circle. Then they clapped their hands over their heads and the dance was over. In Jane's opinion, it had passed exceedingly quickly.

The next dance would not start for several minutes. "Would you like to take some refreshment?" Mr. Lefroy asked. As he took Jane's hand and led her across the room, Jane caught the knowing gaze of Madame Lefroy. Jane tossed her head to discount her friend's suspicions. Dancing with Mr. Lefroy had been a convenience, not part of a greater plan to ensnare his affections, she told herself firmly.

"Here you are," Mr. Lefroy said, handing her a glass of the watered-down wine. They moved to the corner near the window where it was cooler. He took a sip of his own and wrinkled his nose.

"It's not very good, I know," Jane said, immediately annoyed with her apologetic tone.

"Well, what can one expect at a subscription ball?" he asked.

"I apologize if the ball is disappointing," she replied tartly. Apparently he had not enjoyed their dance as much as she had.

His eyes fixed on her, Mr. Lefroy said, "On the contrary: The Basingstoke Assembly Ball is growing in my esteem by the moment."

Jane sipped her wine, unsure how to respond. Suddenly she remembered that she should be keeping a watchful eye on Eliza. She shook her head with annoyance. How could she have let herself get so distracted? She looked around the crowded ballroom; Eliza was nowhere to be seen.

CHAPTER 11

"You must allow that I am not likely to
be deceived as to the name of the man on
whom all my happiness depends."
SENSE AND SENSIBILITY

"Thank you for the dance," Jane said. "If you will excuse me, I must find my cousin."

"Another mysterious assignation?" Mr. Lefroy asked, his eyebrows arched high.

"Don't be ridiculous," she snapped. "My cousin may need me."

His face lost its playfulness, and he stepped back. "Then I must let you go." He bowed from the waist. His speculative look made Jane feel as though he had bested her and she was retreating from the battlefield. Nevertheless, she hurried away, worried for Eliza.

Jane circled the ballroom, distractedly greeting acquaintances. She spied Henry standing in a corner with a group of other officers, drinking and joking. If Eliza was not with him, where was she?

There was James standing by the fire. Dabbing at his forehead with his handkerchief, he was talking earnestly with the Reverend Lefroy, Madame's husband, who was as ponderous as James was.

James beckoned her over. "There you are, Jane. Where is Eliza?" he asked.

"I'm looking for her now," Jane answered.

"I want to claim the next dance with her," he said. "I've been practicing, you know. Henry can't keep her all to himself; it's my turn."

"I'll tell her you asked after her," Jane promised.

Madame Lefroy was sitting near the fire with the other older ladies. As Jane was about to approach her to inquire after Eliza, she caught a glimpse of a flash of yellow muslin across the room. With a quick wave to Madame, she hurried over to the corner, where a discreet door was tucked away behind a potted plant. Eliza must have gone through it.

Behind the door, a stairwell led to the private courtyard of the Assembly Hall. Lit by torches in every corner, the yard was seemingly deserted. Just then a woman cried out. In the farthest corner, Jane saw a woman crumple to the ground. A masculine figure bent over her.

"Eliza!" Jane ran to the spot. Her cousin lay on her back on the cold ground.

Although she had known Eliza would try to meet her mystery man, Jane was still shocked to see him a stone's throw from all the notables of Hampshire. His face was uncovered now, but he had retreated to the shadows when Jane approached. Throwing her arms across Eliza's body to shield her, Jane stared up at the man.

"Stay away from her!" she ordered. He raised his hands as if in surrender.

"Eliza, speak to me," Jane pleaded. Eliza moaned, and Jane let out a breath of relief. She lifted Eliza's head from the ground and cradled it in her lap.

"She is not hurt; only overcome," the man said. "If you will permit me, I will pick her up and bring her somewhere more suitable."

"Don't touch her!" Jane cried. "You have no right."

"I have every right in the world," he said, coming out into the light of the torches. His face was uncovered now, but it was still not familiar to Jane. Except for those eyes. She had seen them before. Who was he?

"What right?" Jane demanded.

"Don't you recognize me, cousin?" the man asked.

Eliza's eyes flickered open. "Jane," she said faintly.

"I'm here," Jane said. "Did this man hurt you?"

"No of course not," Eliza said, her hand to her forehead. "He is my husband."

Jane stared, disbelieving. It couldn't be. Eliza's husband was dead.

The gentleman clicked his heels together and made a low courtly bow. "Miss Austen, Jean Capot de Feuillide, at your service."

After a moment Jane found her voice. "But, sir, we were told you were dead."

"Thankfully, the reports were inaccurate," the Comte said, kneeling at his wife's side. "My dear, can you stand?"

They helped Eliza to her feet and led her to a rough bench against the wall. He sat with her, his arm wrapped protectively about her shoulder.

Eliza's pale face stared up at her resurrected husband. "Is it really you, Jean?"

Jane's eyes went from one to the other. A moment ago, she had assumed Eliza must have known the Comte was alive, but no one could fake Eliza's genuine surprise.

"Sir," Jane began. "How are you here, in Hampshire, when you were supposed to be dead in Paris these past eighteen months?"

"Cousin, call me Jean," he said.

"How is it that you are alive?" she insisted. "And here in Hampshire?"

Before he could answer, the door opened across the courtyard, spilling a rectangle of light across the bare ground. "Miss Austen?"

It was Tom Lefroy. When he spied her across the yard, he hurried toward her. The Comte tensed, ready to flee. Jane held up a hand to reassure him.

"I'll take care of him," she said quietly. She moved quickly to meet Mr. Lefroy in the center of the courtyard. Blocking his way, she asked, "Are you following me, Mr. Lefroy?"

The flickering torchlight picked out the golden highlights in his hair, and the shadows sharpened his cheekbones. "I was concerned when you left the ball so abruptly," he said, but something in his face made Jane suspicious of his motives. He seemed to sense her wariness. "But if you do not require my assistance, I shall go."

While he spoke, Jane saw his eyes searching the shadows behind her and she made a quick decision. "Thank goodness you have come," she said, injecting as much relief as she could into her tone. "My cousin is indisposed. I must take her home. Can you find Henry?"

Surprised, he asked, "The Comtesse? What is wrong?"

He started to move past her toward Eliza, but Jane placed a hand on his arm. "Mr. Lefroy—Tom! Please get my brother! Hurry!"

He stopped. "Of course," he said. She heard a hint of reluctance in his tone, but as a gentleman he could hardly ignore such a direct plea.

Jane waited until he had reentered the Assembly Hall, then she rushed back to Eliza and the Comte. He was whispering quickly in her ear and Eliza was nodding as if in a daze. "I got rid of him, but not for long," Jane warned.

The Comte said, "I must not be seen. No one must know I am alive." His eyes darted about the shadows.

"What are you afraid of?" Jane whispered.

"I must go now!" He brushed Eliza's forehead with a kiss and took Jane's hand. "I am very pleased that my dear Eliza has such a magnificent ally." Then he disappeared into the darkness.

For a moment, Jane allowed herself to enjoy his compliment. But there was no time. She turned to Eliza. "Did you know your husband was alive?"

"Of course not," Eliza said weakly. "I have worn mourning for a year! And you know how I hate how black dulls my complexion."

Despite the gravity of the situation, Jane couldn't keep herself from giggling.

"Eliza!" The door was flung open and Henry's footsteps pounded across the courtyard. "Are you ill?"

Eliza gripped Jane's hand tightly. "You must not tell anyone about Jean!" she whispered.

"I shall keep your secret," Jane promised. "So long as you bring me fully into your confidence."

The arrival of Henry, followed by Tom Lefroy, rescued Eliza from having to answer. The men easily accepted Jane's explanation that Eliza had felt faint and needed to go home. Henry, as befitting an army officer, took charge. Within minutes, Mr. Lefroy had retrieved their coats and Jacques had brought the carriage directly into the courtyard. Effortlessly, Henry carried Eliza into the carriage.

As he was arranging the blankets around her, Jane waited outside. She heard Henry whispering sweet nothings to Eliza; words that were in no way appropriate to say to a married woman. Jane sighed. What would happen to Henry and Eliza now? Equally important, didn't Eliza realize how suspicious it would look to the War Office that her dead husband had suddenly reappeared—alive?

Contemplating Jacques perched on his driver's seat, Jane wondered what he would think of his master's miraculous return. How was it that he had not recognized the Comte on their earlier encounter on the road from Godmersham?

"I hope I was able to be of service," Mr. Lefroy said at her elbow. She started, having forgotten his presence.

"Yes, thank you for fetching my brother," she said. "That was very kind."

"If you would only confide in me, I'm sure I could help you further," he said.

"I beg your pardon?" Jane asked.

"Once again, I've found you in a clandestine meeting with a mysterious man," Mr. Lefroy said. His eyes were bright and interested. "And I thought this ball was going to be dull!"

With a sinking heart, Jane realized that Mr. Lefroy was intrigued.

"Don't deny it, Miss Austen," he went on. "I saw him. It was the same man you met outside the parsonage. I recognized his build and way of moving. But this time he was with your cousin; are you protecting her reputation?"

Jane couldn't help but appreciate the irony; Eliza's secret meeting with a stranger was with her own husband!

"Perhaps I am protecting my own respectability," she said.

"With your independence of mind, you care nothing for the opinion of others," he said. "Who was that gentleman?"

"There was no gentleman," she lied. Her voice, even to herself, lacked conviction. "You saw a shadow and built a fantasy around it."

"Twice? I think not," Lefroy said.

Jane was silent, trying to think of something to say to distract him. She had no reason to trust Mr. Lefroy.

Suddenly, Henry stepped out of the carriage. "Come quickly, Jane," he said, holding out his hand. "I'm worried about Eliza. The sooner we get her home the better."

Mr. Lefroy stepped closer to Jane and with a slight bow said quickly, "I am at your complete disposal should you need my help." She listened for a false note but was forced to admit she heard none. "And you can trust my discretion. There is no reason that anyone else needs to know what I saw."

Jane's breath caught in her throat. Was he threatening to expose her? Or could she accept his offer was sincere? "Thank you, Mr. Lefroy," she said noncommittally. Then she climbed into the carriage, grateful to put a little distance between her and Mr. Tom Lefroy.

Sitting next to Eliza, Jane pulled the blankets around their legs. Until now, Jane hadn't noticed how chilled her hands and feet had become. She pressed her slippers against the heated bricks. Henry hopped into the carriage as well.

"I shall call tomorrow to see how the Comtesse is feeling," Mr. Lefroy promised as he carefully shut the carriage door.

"That won't be necessary," Jane called.

"Nevertheless, you shall see me tomorrow."

As they drove away over the cobblestoned courtyard, Henry said to Jane, "Mr. Lefroy seems very interested in your affairs. I think you've made a conquest there."

Startled, Jane looked at Henry. Had he overheard their conversation? But the expression on his face was teasing, not suspicious.

"With Mr. Lefroy? Heaven forfend," she said. "He is bored. Eliza's indisposition was the only point of interest for him at a dull ball." At least she hoped that was the extent of his interest. She closed her eyes and tried to make sense of her contradictory thoughts and inclinations.

Eliza leaned against the wall of the carriage and lifted her head. "Jane, you underestimate your charms. Mr. Lefroy is smitten, just as his aunt hoped he would be."

"Don't be ridiculous," Jane snapped. Irritated with both of them, she turned to the window. She desperately wanted to talk to Eliza, but Henry's presence constrained her. She would have to wait.

Jane stared out the window; the moon cast a bright light over the snow-covered fields. Although the sky was clear, she thought she could smell snow in the air. James often teased her about her weather sense, but it was nearly infallible.

She sat bolt upright.

"Jane, what is wrong?" Henry asked.

"We forgot James at the ball!"

CHAPTER 12

And his behaviour, so strikingly altered,—
what could it mean? . . . but to speak with such
civility, to inquire after her family! . . .
Never had he spoken with such gentleness
as on this unexpected meeting.
PRIDE AND PREJUDICE

*W*hen Jane woke up the next morning, the first thing she did was to glance at her sister's empty bed and wish Cassandra was there to talk to. The night before, Eliza had avoided any private conversations by summoning Marie as soon as they arrived home. Mrs. Austen had bustled about, making a fuss over Eliza and scolding Jane and Henry for forgetting James at the ball. Jane consoled her mother, assuring her that James would find a ride from any number of neighbors or stay with the Bigg-Withers. Henry had carefully avoided participating in the conversation, and from the smirk on his face, Jane wondered whether he had deliberately left James behind so he could have Eliza to himself. Little did Henry realize that he had a new rival—one who had the advantage of already being married to the lady in question.

Jane had tried to visit Eliza after the household had gone to sleep, but Marie had insisted that her mistress was not to be bothered. And now Eliza would stay abed until at least noon. Perhaps even later, depending on how much she wanted to avoid Jane's questions.

Jane hopped out of bed and dressed quickly in the chilly room. Then she went downstairs, and with only Dame Staples, their cook, for company, she ate a quick breakfast in front of the kitchen fire. Finally, taking advantage of the quiet, she continued her letter to Cassandra.

So you see, Sister, the only terrible thing that ever happened to Eliza is undone. Once she recovers from the considerable shock, she will be overjoyed. Poor Henry, on the other hand, will be left in the cold.

Jane crumpled the paper and tossed it into the fire. Any letter she sent to Cassandra might be intercepted, although she thought it unlikely. The War Office didn't know this secret yet, and until Jane knew more, she would not be the one to tell them.

Why had the Comte kept Eliza in the dark for over a year? And why reveal himself now? Did this have something to do with the War Office's suspicions of Eliza?

She decided she needed some air. It was high time she visited her brother George. The people who cared for him in Deane were country folk and would be awake by the time she arrived. Bundled in her pelisse, warmest bonnet, and fur-lined gloves—the last borrowed from Eliza—Jane left the parsonage.

The road that led from the parsonage was lined with small cottages. The wind gusts tasted of snow, but as yet there were only occasional flurries. All the farmland and fields she could see belonged to the parsonage, and the majority of the villagers worked for her father.

She passed the large kitchen garden and the barn where the Austens kept pigs and chickens. Between them, the Austens were well provided with foodstuffs, but they had very little extra cash, most of which was earmarked for the sons' careers. Jane and Cassandra could count only on their fifty pounds per annum and no dowries at all.

Her thoughts flew to Eliza, fast asleep at the parsonage. In the privacy of her own meditations, Jane could admit how she envied her cousin. Eliza had rank and wealth enough to make her own decisions. Her son was practically an invalid, but Eliza had the means and inclination to keep him at home with her. Her dead husband had been resurrected in the most romantic and mysterious way possible!

Jane longed to live like Eliza did, to the fullest and with verve. Even better, she wished she could transform herself into one of her own heroines and with a stroke of her pen create a perfect match for herself. Someone with enough money that he could choose to marry a penniless girl. And he must dance! But most of all, he must accept Jane for who she was, ink-stained fingers and all.

She shook her head ruefully at her childlike fantasies. Writing would have to be her solace for being an old maid.

Her tragic thoughts were interrupted when she noticed a gentleman walking toward her. Mr. Lefroy! This was too much, too much indeed. Last night he had followed her from the ball, and now he was outside her house before nine o'clock in the morning! What on earth was he doing here? She waited to speak until he had caught her up in the middle of the lane.

"Mr. Lefroy," she said, bobbing in a mild curtsy.

"Miss Austen, I had not dared hope I would see you so early in the day." He bowed.

"It is not the usual time for a call," she said dryly. "Particularly for visitors from Town. I thought Londoners slept till noon."

"Ah, but I am only newly a Londoner. I kept early hours in Ireland," he said. "I thought I should tell you that James spent the night at Ashe Rectory. My aunt insisted, over his objections."

Jane immediately felt contrite. "Was he very put out that we forgot him?"

"He may be under the impression that you did not forget him at all, but that the demands of your cousin's illness kept his party from waiting for him."

"And should I thank you for conveying such an idea into his head?" Jane asked, with a wry smile.

"A bit of improvisation seemed to be called for," he said gallantly.

"I am very grateful," she said. He looked at her with a dubious air. "No, I truly am," she insisted.

"As I told you last night: anything I can do to be of service." He put his hand to his heart. "Brothers rescued, coats fetched, secrets kept—I can do it all."

Jane considered him carefully. Perhaps he had earned a tiny bit of her confidence. "Mr. Lefroy . . ."

"Please, call me Tom."

With a sense of stepping into a level of intimacy she had not anticipated, she said, "Then you must call me Jane. If the secrets you seek were mine, I might tell you one or two. But I cannot betray another's confidences."

"Your cousin, the Comtesse?"

Jane narrowed her eyes. "No matter how artful you are, you shall not convince me to reveal anything more than I already have."

"In that case, shall we walk?" he asked. "Where are you going this very cold morning?"

She eyed him suspiciously. He had given up too easily. "I'm going to Deane to visit . . . a relation."

"That's several miles, isn't it?" he asked, grimacing. "May I accompany you?"

"I am perfectly capable of walking there myself," she said. "As for you—those boots you're wearing may be just the thing in London, but they'll give you blisters after a long walk in the country."

"I'm fine," he assured her.

"Suit yourself," Jane said. "But I am a quick walker."

With a grieved look, he said, "I expected nothing less."

They passed through the tiny village of Steventon, at perhaps a brisker pace than even Jane would usually set. Tom was surprised that there were no shops or inns.

"The nearest public house is in Deane. The post comes there, too," Jane said. "But for our shopping we go to Basingstoke."

"I'm used to having more choices for my entertainment." Tom said.

"London is a feast of diversions," Jane said.

"Yes," he agreed. "But I miss home."

"What is Limerick like?" Jane asked.

He beamed and began to talk. Jane had the sense that he was lonely in the city and had no one to tell his stories to. For the rest of their walk, he amused her with stories of his misadventures growing up and studying law at Trinity College in Dublin. "And now my uncle is supporting my application to the bar."

"The beginning of a promising career," Jane offered. As she knew from her brothers' situations, gentlemen without fortune, however well educated, required patrons to ease their way into their professions.

Tom didn't speak again for a long while. Jane was appreciative of someone who felt no need to talk if he had nothing to say. She found his company unexpectedly restful.

But when they arrived at the outskirts of Deane, she paused in front of the well-kept cottage where her brother lived. "Thank you for accompanying me. Your company has made the time pass very quickly, but I shall take my leave of you now."

Just then, the door of the cottage swung open, and her brother ran out to Jane and hugged her tight. "George!" she cried.

In return, he smiled widely and mouthed "Jane." His sisters were his favorites, in part because they had learned how to speak with their fingers to communicate with him. He could not hear, and that had affected his speech and his understanding. Although he was nearly eleven years older than Jane, his mentality was that of a child.

Over his shoulder, Jane saw a startled Tom step back. She hugged George back and using her hands to echo her spoken word, she said, "George, this is my . . . friend Tom." She wasn't sure whether Tom deserved the title of friend, but it was impossible to explain such nuances to George.

George waved and beamed at Tom. Jane watched, tense, waiting to see whether he might mock her brother's disabilities.

Tom smiled at Jane and then turned to George. To her shock, Tom began to speak with his hands as well. He had his own way of communicating his words, but Jane recognized enough to understand that Tom was saying he was pleased to meet George and that he admired George's sister greatly.

Practically bouncing up and down with excitement, George signed his welcome to Tom. Then he ran into the house, pausing at the door to beckon them inside.

"Is it because of George's condition that you didn't want me here?" Tom asked quietly.

"Yes," Jane answered honestly. "I didn't think you would understand or sympathize."

"One of my sisters is deaf," he said simply.

As Jane preceded him through the narrow doorway, she was thoughtful. Perhaps she had been too hasty when she had decided she thoroughly disliked Mr. Tom Lefroy.

CHAPTER 13

*"I have had my doubts, I confess; but
they are fainter than they were, and they
may soon be entirely done away."*
SENSE AND SENSIBILITY

$\mathcal{B}$y the time Jane and Tom left the cottage, the scattered flurries had settled into a gently falling snow.

"I'll come back soon," Jane promised George, her fingers fluttering rapidly in the air.

"If I may, I will visit again too," Tom said.

George solemnly shook hands with Tom, but when he turned to Jane, he streaked his fingers down his face.

"Does that mean he's sad?" Tom asked.

"Yes. Those are tears," Jane said. She embraced her brother, letting him squeeze her tightly for as long as he wished. As they walked away, Jane glanced back to see him waving hard, and vowed to visit more often.

"What shall we do now? I believe there is an establishment that calls itself an inn in Deane. A cup of tea perhaps?" Tom asked brightly, as though they had planned to spend the day together.

"I have to get home," Jane said.

Disregarding her refusal, he went on, "But now that we know each other better, it would be the perfect opportunity to tell me all about your mysterious noble cousin."

Jane stared. Eliza's situation had been so much on her mind that for a moment she thought he was referring to the Comte.

Tom noticed her confusion and, mistaking it for irritation, said, "Please, don't let my curiosity about the fair Comtesse keep us from being friends. On second thought, we need not discuss her at all."

Relieved, Jane quickly answered, "There is really little to say about my cousin that you don't already know. I must go. My mother will be expecting me for breakfast."

"That's something I miss in London," Tom confided. "In the country you can do a dozen things before breakfast." He shifted on feet that were clearly sore. "We mustn't keep your mother waiting. Let me escort you home."

Thinking of Tom's sore feet, Jane chuckled. "That will take you miles out of your way." She pointed. "Ashe is due west. I am perfectly capable of walking back on my own."

Before Tom could politely protest, a solution appeared on the road. Jane immediately recognized Jacques in the driver's seat of Eliza's carriage. "Good morning, Jacques," she called.

He touched his cap, then his chest, reminding her of the odd gesture she had seen the Comte do on their first meeting. "Mademoiselle," he said.

"Are you on an errand for my cousin?" she asked.

"I've just collected my mistress's mail," he answered. "Your mother asked me to collect the household's, too."

"I'll take it," Jane said, holding her hand up to him. She was expecting a letter from Cassandra.

Jacques scowled and hesitated.

"Is there something the matter?" she asked, wondering at his odd behavior.

"The lady asked for the post," Tom said, his voice filled with peremptory command. He held out his gloved hand. Jacques stared down at him and reluctantly handed the mail over. But Jane caught a glimpse of the heavy paper with an official red seal that Jacques held back and tucked away in his coat.

In the small pile were several letters addressed to Eliza, prompting Jane to wonder which letter Jacques had held back if it wasn't one for his mistress. Surely no one who could afford paper like that would be writing to a coachman.

Tom opened his mouth to reprimand Jacques, but Jane shook her head. Jacques was Eliza's servant, not hers.

"Jacques, I will ride back to Steventon with you," Jane announced. She turned to Tom. "If you go down this road, you'll be in Ashe in twenty minutes. I am glad we had this opportunity to talk."

"As am I, Jane." A smile played across his lips. "My aunt told me that you were the only tolerable girl in the county. She was right."

Jane shook her head in mock sadness. "Just as I was beginning to think you were an actual gentleman, you mock me. I must assure you Hampshire is full of young ladies far more tolerable than myself."

"I doubt that very much." With a cheeky grin, Tom bowed and held open the door to the carriage. "Good day, Miss Austen," he said, speaking formally for the benefit of the servant's ears.

"Good day, Mr. Lefroy," she said.

As they headed back to the parsonage, Jane was quite relieved to have the carriage. She wouldn't have admitted it to Tom Lefroy for a hundred pounds, but her toes felt frozen solid. She thought again of poor Tom in his city boots.

Should she have offered him a ride? But it would have been so forward, and the carriage wasn't even her own. Besides, she hadn't invited him to walk with her to begin with!

She thumbed through the letters, pleased to see one from Cassandra. She ripped it open and scanned the contents quickly.

Cassandra had written a full page about the antics of their nieces and nephews but only a few lines about Edward and his surveillance of Eliza. "Our brother has frequent meetings with your mysterious Major Smythe," Cassandra had written. "I gave the footman a shilling to tell me whenever he comes, and tried to overhear their conversations but was immediately discovered. Sister, I lack your ability to eavesdrop successfully." Jane smiled at the thought of her forthright sister trying to listen at keyholes. "So unfortunately, I am none the wiser than I was before." That was too bad, Jane thought. She had so much news to report—if only she dared write! Cassandra would be quite jealous.

Quite soon the carriage rumbled up the gravel path in front of the parsonage. Jacques leapt down and opened the carriage door for her.

"Thank you, Jacques," she said, stepping down onto the drive. He waited for her to go inside, but she hesitated. How much did he know about Eliza's affairs? In Jane's experience the servants always knew everything.

"Do you remember that gesture I asked you about on the ride home from Godmersham?"

Jacques' leathery face was impassive. "I cannot recall, mademoiselle."

Jane frowned. "This." She repeated the Comte's salute, touching her forehead, then her lips. "Surely you remember?"

"Perhaps," Jacques said, his eyes fixed on a point somewhere above her head.

"Tell me, is that a French habit?"

He shrugged. "It is common in the Landes, where I am from."

"So that is why you were surprised to see it?" she pressed.

"Oui. Why else, mademoiselle?" he asked. In vain, Jane searched his impassive face for any hint of his true feelings.

"I thought perhaps it was something your late master used to do," she said. "It must have been quite a shock to lose him that way."

He shot her a surprised glance, then a look of deep sadness passed across his face. "It was," he answered flatly.

Eyes narrowed, Jane nodded and went inside. Jacques was keeping something secret, certainly, but she didn't think he knew about the Comte's miraculous resurrection. Otherwise, he would not be so grieved.

Jane handed her coat and gloves to Prudence and started for the parlor. She immediately saw that, despite the fire blazing merrily, the atmosphere in the house was as frigid as it was outside. Jane tried to back out of the room before she was noticed, but a preemptory call from her mother put an end to that plan.

"Where have you been, Jane?" Mrs. Austen's eyes were full of relief. She was ensconced on her couch, mending the household linen, but Jane could easily see that all her mother's attention was on the two feuding sons next to her.

"There you are, sister," James said from the armchair in the corner. "As you can see, I arrived home safely even though my own relations abandoned me in Basingstoke."

"James, stop whining. It ill becomes a man of the cloth to be so petty," Henry said from his armchair close to the fire.

Injecting as much warmth into her voice as she could, Jane said, "James, when Eliza was feeling faint last night, I knew I could depend on you to make your own way home."

"I don't blame *you*, Jane," James said, glaring at Henry. "You were merely trying to care for our cousin."

Before Henry and James could start again, she said, "Excuse me, I left my book upstairs."

"No you didn't, dear," her mother said. "It's right here."

Jane wanted to pull out her hair. She had a genuine mystery to solve but instead she was trapped in the drawing room playing peacemaker. If only Eliza would wake up!

She moved to the pianoforte in the window bay overlooking the garden. She could see Jacques chopping wood. He was quite expert; his ax cleaved the wood with one blow. Idly watching him, she rearranged her sheets of music, all carefully copied from friends to save the cost of purchasing. She sighed at the snow coming down more heavily than before. There would be no visitors today. If Eliza planned to meet her husband, the weather would surely prevent such a rendezvous. Jane picked out a melody, enjoying the counterpoint with the thud of the axe outside.

Suddenly her attention was drawn by a glimpse of color and movement in the garden. She stopped playing to watch. A woman in a dark cloak was picking her way around the empty flower beds. Was it Eliza?

As Jane watched, the woman went to Jacques. The hood fell back onto the woman's shoulders and Jane saw it wasn't Eliza at all but Marie, her maid.

As Marie spoke, she gestured sharply with her hands. Jacques caught her wrist. Jane tensed, wondering whether Jacques meant her harm, but then she relaxed as Marie put her hand to Jacques' cheek. She spoke rapidly, and he seemed to be appeased. He returned to his chopping while Marie disappeared into the woods.

Interesting, Jane thought. The intrigue around Eliza even extended to her servants.

"Are you going to play or just stare out the window?" Henry asked.

Jane glared at him. "Since you will nap regardless of what I do, I don't see that it matters," she retorted.

"Children, stop squabbling," Mrs. Austen scolded without looking up from her mending. "Jane, just play."

Jane selected a cheerful jig and started playing the pianoforte with enough energy, she hoped, to wake the dead.

"Jane, it's early," her mother called over the music. "A little less exuberance if you please."

"A jig, I see. That Lefroy fellow is from Limerick, isn't he?" Henry asked knowingly. "I don't wonder that an Irish tune is your new favorite."

"I don't know what you could possibly be referring to," Jane rejoined. "I don't care sixpence for Mr. Lefroy!" She pushed herself away from the piano and stomped to the hall. Through the door to the kitchen she spied Prudence preparing a tray for the only member of the household still abed.

"Is this for the Comtesse?" Jane asked.

"Yes," Prudence said. "And it should be her ladyship's maid who fetches it, but that French girl is nowhere to be found!"

"I'll bring it up," Jane offered and took it from the table up the backstairs. She tapped at Eliza's door. There was a brief silence, then Eliza's voice warily asked, "Yes?"

"Tea, ma'am." Jane deliberately roughened her voice to sound like Prudence's.

"Oh, come in."

When Jane entered, Eliza was standing at the window. As Jane had half-expected, Eliza was wide awake and fully dressed.

"Good morning!" Jane said cheerfully.

Eliza jerked round to face her. Jane was distressed to see how pale and pinched her cousin's face was. "Jane!" she exclaimed. "Why are you bringing me breakfast? The Austens aren't economizing on the servants again, are they?" Her attempt at levity didn't disguise her dismay.

"We're always economizing, but that is not why I'm here. I need to talk to you," Jane said simply. "And since you refuse to come downstairs . . ."

"That's absurd. I had a sleepless night, and I am not yet fit for company." She glanced at the door, her unspoken wish for Jane to leave very clear.

"You've been avoiding me," Jane accused. "But we have to talk."

"Later, Jane."

"No. You must tell me everything now. I can't keep your secrets if you refuse to confide in me."

"Isn't a secret best kept by telling no one?" Eliza asked. A few days earlier, the question would have been spirited, but now Eliza seemed merely desperate.

"You need my help," Jane insisted. "Whatever your husband said to you last night—whatever he asked you to do—is worrying you to death. Let me help you."

"I cannot," Eliza said, twisting her wedding ring over and over again on her finger.

Jane thought it might be a good tactic to come at Eliza from a different angle. "I saw Marie outside earlier."

Eliza did not seem interested. "She doesn't like snow. How unaccountable."

"She spoke with Jacques. They seem to be close. Are they friends? Is there a romance in the offing?"

"Brother and sister," Eliza said.

"I don't see any resemblance," Jane said, trying to reconcile this new information with her impressions of Jacques and Marie.

Eliza shook her head. "They are brother and sister-in-law. Marie's husband, René, the one who died, was Jacques' brother."

"So René did die?"

"Of course he did."

"Eliza, there is no 'of course' about it! Your husband was supposed to be dead, too."

Eliza pursed her lips and shook her head. "I don't want to discuss it."

"You must." Jane was implacable. "Unless you want me to tell Edward, who will surely tell the War Office . . ."

"You mustn't," Eliza cried.

"Then tell *me*."

Eliza pulled a shawl around her shoulder and perched on a chair next to the small fire. She stared into the flames for several moments. Finally she turned to Jane with a pale echo of her usual cheerfulness. "We had such a romantic tale, you see."

"I was a child; I don't really recall the details," Jane said. "Why don't you tell me the whole story?"

"My mother brought me to Paris instead of doing my season here," Eliza began. "Everything was so wonderful— the parties, the salons, the clothes! It was magical. And the Comte was always there. He had a title, which impressed Mama. And he was so handsome and so urbane. He began courting me almost immediately. It was so easy to think I was in love."

"You weren't?" Jane asked. Eliza's mystique had always been intertwined with her romantic past.

"Infatuated. Swept up in the moment. Before I knew it we were married—but he was so much older than I."

"That doesn't preclude affection, does it?"

"No—but we had little in common. And I never saw him. He was always at his estate in the Landes. His obsession was a water project to drain the swamps and reclaim the land for farming. I never understood it. But I think he came to Paris to find a rich bride to finance the work."

"Oh, Eliza!" The words wafted out on a wave of sympathy. Jane had never suspected.

"Don't pity me," Eliza said, suddenly fierce. "I was no worse off than many an English matron. Possibly I was even lucky. My husband hardly bothered with me. And then I had my son for solace. I made my life here while he was in France. Until . . ."

"Until he was imprisoned and guillotined," Jane finished. "Or so we thought."

"And now he is back," Eliza said.

"Did you know he was alive?"

"No!" Eliza cried. "The French papers reported his death. The English government confirmed it. Why would I doubt that?"

"So you did not know that it was he who would meet you at the ball?"

Eliza shook her head.

"Then who did you expect to see?" Jane asked. "What did that note say?"

"It said I was to come to the courtyard after the first dance. A friend would be there and he would have news of my husband. It was signed '*J*', but I never dreamed . . ."

Jane had to force herself not to sound suspicious. "Didn't you recognize Jean's handwriting?"

Eliza shrugged. "He wrote to me so rarely. I hoped he had arranged to deliver a last message to me. To his son. Instructions perhaps." She went to the window and stared at the snow falling. The room was silent except for the crackle of the fire.

"And when you saw it was Jean himself?" Jane prompted.

"I was . . . overcome," Eliza said faintly. "I've been a widow for more than a year."

"And a merry one at that," Jane murmured. Eliza pursed her lips.

"I'm sorry," Jane said contritely. "You did not know. But what does he want now?"

Instead of answering, Eliza went to the fire and shifted the embers with a poker.

"Eliza?"

"I don't know."

Jane paced about the room. Had Jean de Feuillide delayed returning to his wife because he did not trust her? No, that was absurd. For all her French affections, Eliza was English to the bone. If anyone was a French spy it was Jean. But why? A French nobleman had all his fortune and estates to regain if the English won the war.

"He must have said something," Jane pressed.

Eliza faced Jane, and there was a determination in the upward tilt of her chin. Her expression was no longer the frivolous one that Jane was accustomed to. By a trick of the winter light, her blue eyes had turned slate gray. Jane could see that Eliza was resolved to keep her secrets.

CHAPTER 14

"The whole of his behavior," replied Elinor,
"from the beginning to the end of the affair,
has been grounded on selfishness . . ."
"It is very true. My happiness never was his object."
SENSE AND SENSIBILITY

$\mathscr{T}$he afternoon spun out tediously. The snow fell more thickly, blanketing the garden, the fields, and the road. The parlor's fire—stoked periodically by Jacques, who had a knack for making himself useful indoors and out—kept the room close and warm. Henry and James had vied for Eliza's attention for a while but they eventually fell into a doze. Mrs. Austen napped, and little ladylike snuffles emanated from the couch, competing with James's masculine snoring.

Eliza read her novel, while Jane wrote hers. A typical winter afternoon, except for Eliza's tendency to watch the clock on the mantel. A most un-Eliza-like habit, Jane thought. Unless Eliza was late for a party, she never had the faintest idea of the time.

Eliza's agitation worsened as the hour of four o'clock drew near. Jane could hardly contain her curiosity. Did the Comte intend to come calling? Surely he had not hidden himself so carefully to then just walk up to the Austens' front door? Perhaps he was waiting in the garden. Jane dared not go to the window and look, lest she reveal her suspicions to Eliza. But how could Eliza sneak out to see him without alerting Jane?

Jane decided to give Eliza the opportunity she was sure her cousin was looking for. She yawned and put her pen down. After blotting the paper, she slipped it inside her writing desk. "I cannot keep my eyes open," she said. "I followed last night's exertions with a long walk to Deane this morning."

"Why don't you lie down for a little while?" Eliza suggested. Her casual tone was belied by the sudden tension in her body.

"I wouldn't want to leave you alone. The rest of the Austens are poor company this afternoon."

"Jane, family need make no apologies. I'll finish my book and then come upstairs for a sleep, too." She smiled at Jane. "I insist!"

"Very well," Jane said, marveling at Eliza's duplicity.

Once in her room, Jane hurriedly put on an old pair of boots and bundled up in her warmest layers, as well as an old white shawl of Cassandra's she hoped would disguise her in the snow. She slipped out of her room and tiptoed down the servants' stairs. Shushing the cook and Prudence, she peeked out the kitchen door to see Eliza in the hall, justifying all of Jane's worst suspicions. Eliza pulled on her dark fur-lined pelisse and slipped out the garden door into the wintry whiteness.

Jane followed Eliza up the deserted lane that led from the parsonage to Reverend Austen's church. Jane wasn't surprised. The church was a quarter mile beyond the village and stood empty for six days of the week; it was a perfect place for a clandestine meeting.

Jane's footsteps were muffled by snow underfoot. An unexpected noise made her jerk her head to see whether she was herself being followed, but she could make out no one in the falling snow.

Jane continued forward, staying to one side of the line of poplars that bordered the path. The bare branches were heavy with snow. She told herself that a pile of snow falling to the ground must have been the cause of the alarming thud.

Jane stopped only when she spied Eliza at the church door. Eliza paused and turned to look backward. Jane kept herself perfectly still, trusting her cousin's weak eyes could not distinguish the white shawl from the snow.

After a moment, Eliza turned and reached for the door-knob. To Jane's surprise, the church door was unlocked even though Eliza hadn't stopped to get the key from its not-so-secret hiding place in an ancient yew tree nearby. Jane drew in her breath sharply as she realized the significance. Eliza must have told the Comte where to find the key. He was already inside.

Suddenly filled with foreboding, Jane raced to the church door. The last time Eliza had seen her husband, she had fainted. Luckily, Eliza had not shut the door completely and Jane was able to slip into the square entryway beneath the bell tower. The church had not changed since medieval times, and on either side of the entry hung the bell ropes; Jane was careful not to brush against them in passing.

"How could you not tell me you were alive?" Eliza's voice was angry. "Did you not think of me even once?"

Jane let out a relieved sigh. Eliza wasn't overcome; she was angry. Much safer.

Jane could make out their silhouettes near the light of the fireplace in the middle of the north wall. She crept down the nave, crouching by the end of the pews to avoid being seen.

"Don't be angry, ma chérie. I was trying to protect you." The Comte's wheedling voice was a far cry from the confident highwayman Jane had first met. "On my honor, it was the only way."

"Honor!" Eliza spat the word at him like a bullet. "Was it honorable to abandon us? And what about your creditors?

Once your death was reported, they descended upon me. I paid hundreds of pounds to rid myself of them."

"If you had only paid them while I was alive, then I would not have been in debt," the Comte said bitterly. "I was humiliated when you advertised that you would not be responsible for my obligations."

Jane listened, both aghast and enthralled. Eliza's perfect life had apparently been a lie from beginning to end. She moved closer to hear better, but she stumbled against the end of a pew. She caught the carved armrest to steady herself.

"Who's there?" the Comte said sharply.

Straightening up, Jane moved forward. "It is I," she said.

"Jane?" Eliza asked. "You followed me." She moved forward to meet Jane in the center of the nave. "How could you?" Jane winced at the hurt in Eliza's voice.

"I was worried for you," Jane whispered urgently.

"Very well. Now you know I am safe—just meeting my suddenly resurrected husband. Go home."

"I cannot leave you here, Eliza. I . . ."

Eliza's face was gray and drawn; she looked a decade older than she was. "Jane, our conversation is a personal and private one. You should go."

"She should stay," the Comte said loudly. "We may need her help."

Eliza frowned and whispered, "Cousin, we'll discuss your gross discourtesy later."

"Cousin Jane," the Comte said with a return of his old manner. "It seems to be our fate that you are intertwined in our affairs."

Jane eyed him warily. A blanket spread out on a pew was apparently his bed, and she spied a shaving kit and basin. It was rather remarkable that the Comte could maintain his bravado in such circumstances!

"I care deeply for Eliza," Jane said in her most pointed manner. "And your reappearance, miraculous as it seems, worries me greatly. For Eliza's sake."

"Bien sûr," he said. "Your devotion is admirable."

Jane opened her mouth but was forestalled by Eliza, who said, surprisingly, "Jane and I need no compliments. We want answers. What happened to you a year ago?"

"And where have you been all this time?" Jane added. "And why have you returned?"

"Very well," he said. "It began eighteen months ago. The new regime was making my position impossible. I could not stay with my beloved Eliza here in England if I wanted to keep my estate, so I returned to France."

"You hated it here," Eliza said. "You always wanted to return to your precious building project. You cared more for your dams and canals than me."

"But I did it for you," he insisted. "If I can drain the swamps, I'll be able to cultivate ten thousand hectares. I'll be the richest man in the Landes."

Jane noticed that despite the Comte's changed circumstances, he still appeared to believe his estates were intact. Eliza soon disabused him. "My dear husband, your beloved estate is gone, confiscated by the government. Your project will never come to pass. You've wasted your fortune and years of work on a fruitless quest!" The Comte shot his wife a look so vicious that Jane moved closer to Eliza.

"What happened a year ago?" Jane asked to lessen the tension.

"I was summoned to Paris to account for my management of the peasants on the estate. Someone had informed against me." Jane had heard such incidents were all too common these days in France. The peasants were taking their revenge for centuries of servitude. The fear of the same thing happening in England was what drove the actions of men like her brother and Major Smythe.

"I was warned that I might be arrested, so I devised a stratagem to trick the authorities. I had René wear my clothes and take my place at the hotel. When the police came, he was arrested instead of me."

"You offered up your servant in your place?" Jane asked slowly, unable to hide her contempt.

"I never expected him to be executed!" the Comte insisted. "I thought he would be detained for a few days. Just long enough for me to return safely to England."

"You killed him as surely as if you manned the guillotine yourself," Eliza said.

"That was not my intention," the Comte blustered. "I underestimated how dangerous the new regime was. And after his death . . . well, I had a family to think of."

"And what about poor Marie and her son?" Eliza cried. "You sacrificed her family without a thought."

"Marie and the boy were safe here," he said, averting his eyes from Eliza. Jane wondered that he seemed embarrassed by the only thing he had done that did not reflect badly upon him.

"So, you preserved your own life, no matter the mortal cost," Jane said flatly. "Then why not return to England and your family?"

"I was afraid the danger would follow me here," he said. "I was protecting Eliza."

"That makes no sense," Jane snapped. "The arm of the French government does not stretch across the Channel."

To Jane's surprise, Eliza spoke in her husband's defense. "No, Jane, the French have agents here. He might have been in danger, even in London." She turned back to her husband. "But I have powerful relatives. We could have asked for help."

He shook his head. "If I asked the English government for help, they would want to use me against my countrymen."

Grudgingly, Jane had to agree.

"I am a gentleman," the Comte declared. "I could not debase myself so."

"I hardly think you could sink any lower," Eliza said.

The Comte was silent. After a long moment, Eliza asked, "But why not send me word? It would have been kinder. And you know I can be relied upon."

"I tried," he insisted. "I sent you a letter, signing René's name, asking you to meet me. You never came."

Eliza caught her breath and glanced at Jane. She nodded. That was the letter that Edward had shown Jane.

"Then I became afraid your mail was being intercepted," he said. "I could trust no one. Not even my old servants."

Jane recalled how Jacques had kept a letter from her that morning. Had Eliza been nurturing a spy within her own household?

"Our servants?" Eliza asked.

"In France the peasants were killing their lords." He lowered his gaze. "What if Jacques decided to revenge his brother's death?"

"If he did, he would be completely justified," Eliza said bitterly.

The chill in the church was working its way under Jane's gloves, and she could see that Eliza's teeth were chattering. She added another log to the fire. The small grate gave off hardly any heat, but Jane held her hands out to the flames anyway. The Comte leaned against a stone column without speaking.

"Where did you go?" Jane asked to break the uncomfortable silence.

"Yes, tell us, Jean, where did you cower for all this time?" Eliza asked contemptuously.

The Comte's face clouded in anger, but with a visible effort, he checked his temper. "I went east. To Italy. Greece. Turkey. Wherever I could be out of France's reach."

"So while I was mourning your death, you were frivoling in exotic ports?" Eliza asked.

"Not at all, Eliza. I had very little money. I had to live by my wits. Luckily, I had some valuables to sell to finance my . . . journey."

"Valuables?' Eliza's tone sharpened. "Do you mean my jewels?"

Jane held up a hand before their bickering made intelligent conversation impossible. "Why have you returned?" she asked.

"I have arranged a refuge in America for us," he said, straightening up.

"*Us?*" Eliza asked, her perfect eyebrows lifting in disdain. "*Now* you care about me and Hastings?"

"America?" Jane asked, dismayed. The former colony was so far away.

"Yes, I had some business interests there. I have returned to collect my family for the trip to Boston. The French government cannot touch us there."

"But my life is here," Eliza protested. "My family, my friends."

"We will make new friends." The Comte kneeled in front of Eliza; his voice became husky. "With your charm and beauty, you will conquer America in no time at all."

Eliza touched the short curls at her neck, a sure sign that she was feeling flattered.

Jane's thoughts were in a state of confusion. "There must be another option than America. It is so far away."

"Cousin Jane," the Comte scolded. "This is not your choice to make. Eliza's place is with her husband. Our son needs his father."

Eliza's lovely eyes clouded with indecision. "I must think of Hastings," she murmured. "Could we bring our servants? He is used to his nanny. And what about Marie?"

The Comte's face contorted for a moment. It was so quick that Jane thought it might be a trick of the flickering light from the fireplace. "We can discuss it, certainly," he said. "But would Marie want to come? She may blame me for her husband's death."

"And rightly so," Jane cried. "It is cruel to ask Eliza or Marie to go anywhere with you."

"Jane, please mind your own business," Eliza said sharply. "I need to think of my family."

The Comte rubbed his hands together. "Excellent," he said. "If we are to emigrate, my dear, first you must sell the house and convert all your holdings into cash."

"Cash?" Eliza whispered. "So that's why you've returned."

Jane felt a wave of pity for her cousin.

To Jane's satisfaction, Eliza faced her husband. Her last illusions about him shattered like glass on the stone floor. "You want money. Not me. Not your son."

"I want what belongs to me," he said.

"And if I refuse?" Eliza asked.

"Then I'll take Hastings!" he shouted.

Eliza took a step toward him, her fists clenched. Jane thought she looked like an avenging angel. "Leave my son out of this," she ordered. "Or I'll kill you myself."

The Comte involuntarily took a step back. "Don't be melodramatic. I want all three of us to be together," he said. "We can live like royalty in America." Suddenly impatient, he barked, "You are my wife and you will do as I say!"

"No, I am your widow," Eliza said with finality. "Go to America by yourself." She turned to Jane. "Will you accompany me home, please?"

Jane grabbed Eliza's arm.

"Eliza!" he cried. "Come back! What will I do without you?" The desperation in his voice made Jane pause, but Eliza pulled her forward.

"Eliza! Cousin Jane!" he cried. "You can't abandon me! You are killing me!"

Eliza turned around briefly. "You forget, you are already dead, my dear," she said. Then she closed the door on his pleas and hurried with Jane out into the darkening afternoon.

CHAPTER 15

"But now she is of age, and may choose for
herself; and a pretty choice she has made!"
SENSE AND SENSIBILITY

*T*he brilliant white of the snowy landscape had turned
ominously gray. The snow had stopped, but the thick clouds
in the sky augured more to come. The walk home was quiet.
Eliza drew her hood over her hair so Jane couldn't see her
face. Several times Jane began to speak, but stopped herself.

What could she possibly say? On the one hand, she loved
Eliza and could hardly bear to think that she would never
see her again. But she had been thinking on the long trek

home. Eliza was bound to the Comte, for better or worse. To leave him would be to embroil Eliza in a scandal from which the Austens might never recover. Jane had to consider the futures of her brothers and sister. And her own. Eliza had a fortune; the Austens did not.

They were at the gate to the parsonage before Eliza broke the silence. She spoke in a low voice without looking at Jane.

"Do you think I should go to America?" She sniffed and shook her head a bit, as though she were trying to clear her mind. Jane saw the tears on her cheeks. "What do I owe Jean?"

Jane's hand on the gate latch dropped. "He is still your husband," she said, appealing to Eliza's sense of duty.

Eliza turned to Jane and clasped Jane's hands in hers tightly. Her fingers were ice cold. "But he has behaved despicably. I don't want to go. He is wrong to ask me to."

"But the disgrace . . ." Jane started to say.

"Is mine to bear." Eliza pushed open the gate.

"And your son's," Jane reminded her.

"Hastings . . ." Eliza's voice caught. "We both know that his life is likely to be short."

Jane was silent; Eliza did know how to confront unpleasant truths after all.

Eliza continued, "I won't take him away from everything he knows and loves to please Jean. My husband forfeited his rights when he faked his death."

"But he still has his rights," Jane argued, "under the law and in the church."

"Enough, Jane!" Eliza cried.

The sound of thudding hooves in the gloom was a welcome distraction. "Who would venture out on such a day?" Eliza asked.

A rider, heavily laden, came trotting down the road from Ashe. Before they could make out his features, his cheerful greeting informed them of his identity.

"Hello, ladies of Steventon!" It was Tom Lefroy.

"Tom, what are you doing here in such weather?" Jane asked.

"Tom?" Eliza murmured. "First names already?"

Jane felt her face redden.

Tom reined in his horse. Looking down at them, he grinned. "I've come bearing gifts! My dear aunt took pity on me. After an entire day with only the library and my dreary uncle for company, she knew I was going slowly mad. One of Uncle's parishioners gifted him half a dozen pheasants, and the Austens shall receive their share." He handed down a sack with the bird carcasses.

Eliza laughed. "Madame Lefroy made you carry this on horseback? I don't think pity is what she took on you! More like you must pay for your pleasure."

Tom swung down from the horse. "The road was terrible. Blast this snow. Oh, I beg your pardon."

"I have heard much worse," Eliza said with a flirtatious smile. "Let us go inside—you must be cold."

"And I must inform Cook that we are changing the dinner menu," Jane added.

The evening was a great success. Mrs. Austen presided over a dinner table filled with young people laughing and joking. Jane had not seen her mother so animated since the Austen sons had left home; she was in her element with a large group to manage.

Only once did the atmosphere around the table grow tense. It was James who precipitated an awkward conversation. He sat at the head of the table while their father was away at Oxford. Turning to Henry, he said, "So, brother, I see there's to be an execution in Newhaven next week."

Jane and Mrs. Austen exchanged worried looks. James was referring to a mutiny of officers that had taken place in December. Henry's regiment was involved.

Henry scowled. "As you know, James, I wasn't there. Luckily I was in Oxford."

"In my opinion," Tom said, "the officers received their just deserts. They disobeyed their superior officers and they incited a riot."

"To think only of the result and not the reason is to overlook crucial facts," Jane argued. Her mother winced, but Jane continued. "Those soldiers were billeted in Newhaven for the winter without enough food or shelter or fuel. They have put their lives on the line to protect our country. The very least we can do is feed them."

"Well said, Jane!" Henry said.

Even Mrs. Austen couldn't completely disapprove; she had wept for the poor hungry soldiers, seeing her sons' faces on each one of theirs.

"But that's no excuse for what they did," Tom insisted. "If they were tried in a civilian court, the mitigating circumstances could be considered. But these officers were tried by a military tribunal."

"A merciless tribunal," Jane corrected. "I don't think they should be shot for demanding proper food and shelter."

Tom smiled indulgently, and Jane wanted to slap him. "Such a feminine perspective. Compassion has no place in the courtroom."

"The law is a harsh mistress, then," Jane said. "One whom I don't particularly care for."

"Mother," James said hurriedly, "if you would like to take the ladies into the parlor . . ."

"James, don't be so dull!" Mrs. Austen replied. "The men can join us now. Bring your port and we'll play cards."

James looked put out, but Henry and Tom said they were delighted. Mrs. Austen led the way into the parlor.

"Jane, dear, the fire has gone down. Can you send for more wood?"

"Of course, Mother." Jane went into the kitchen and found the servants were just setting the table for their own dinner. Jacques and Marie were standing to one side, holding themselves aloof from the English servants. Jane wondered what they would say if they knew their former master was still alive and so near.

"Jacques, would you please bring in some of that wood I saw you splitting this morning?"

"Of course, mademoiselle."

Marie's face was peaked, and Jane wondered if she were ill. "Are you all right?" she asked.

"I have a mal de tête," Marie admitted, touching her forehead. "But I am sure that I will feel better after le dîner."

Jane nodded. "I will let the Comtesse know. I'm sure she can change for dinner without you."

"Merci, mademoiselle."

Jane rejoined the others in the parlor. Jacques built up the fire so its merry warmth made nonsense of the falling snow outside. Every so often a gust of wind buffeted the windows.

"Lefroy, you'll have to stay the night," Henry said. "You can't make it home in this weather."

"If I must," Tom said with a resigned smile. He turned to catch Jane staring at him. He winked, and she turned away, hoping the heat of the fire explained the blush on her face.

Soon a whist table was set up. Mrs. Austen, Henry, Eliza, and James completed the quartet. James became more cheerful as he won hand after hand. Jane smiled to herself; her brother's sermons might be dull, but his mathematical skills were sharp.

Henry and Eliza were too busy flirting to even notice their mounting losses. Eliza laughed so gaily at one of Henry's jokes that she needed to dab tears from her eyes with one of her lacy handkerchiefs. Henry surreptitiously palmed the handkerchief and tucked it inside his waistcoat. Jane watched their growing intimacy with dismay.

Tom seated himself beside her. She smiled, welcoming the distraction. "After their card game, perhaps you will read your work for us?" he asked.

Jane shook her head. "I don't think so. It's unfair to impose my scribbles on a group marooned here. No one can escape."

"I've read one of your stories," he confided. "And I assure you, no one would willingly miss the ending."

Stiffening, Jane stared straight ahead. "Which story?" she managed to ask casually.

"A novel of letters between two sisters. *Elinor and Marianne*," he said. "My aunt said you had given her a draft."

"That was too bad of her," Jane said, hiding how much she wanted to know his opinion. "She knew that I did not intend for anyone else to read it."

"I was persistent; don't blame her," Tom said earnestly. "I enjoyed it very much."

She relaxed, and they talked of her story until a burst of laughter from the card table drew their attention. Eliza was glowing. And Henry was hanging on her every word.

"Theirs is a courtship that is proceeding well," Tom said.

Jane was silent. Eliza should know better than to make Henry fall in love with her so easily. Nothing but pain would come from her behavior.

"What is wrong, Jane?" Tom asked. "Do you not think them a good match?"

"I think they are a disastrous pair."

Tom's face was puzzled. "I don't understand," he said. "There's no impediment to the match, is there?" He leaned forward. "Her husband is dead. She has a fortune. Your brother is clearly infatuated."

"There is indeed an impediment," Jane muttered.

Just then, Eliza and Henry excused themselves from the card table.

"I need some air!" Eliza exclaimed. Henry followed at her heels. *Like a lapdog*, Jane thought bitterly. Henry was so eager to be with Eliza he didn't even put his coat on.

Jane tried to remain composed, but fidgeted in her seat, unresponsive to any conversational overtures from Tom. What were Henry and Eliza doing outside for so long? Whatever it was, it was not likely to reflect well on either of them.

"Excuse me, please," Jane said, standing up abruptly and following her brother and cousin out into the garden. At first she didn't see them, but then heard a low laughing from the ramshackle gazebo. Peering into the snow, she made out Eliza and Henry in a passionate embrace.

CHAPTER 16

The event was so shocking, that there were
moments even when her heart revolted from it as
impossible—when she thought it could not be.
MANSFIELD PARK

ap, tap. Jane's discreet knock at Eliza's door was the only sound in the still house.

Jane glanced at the clock in the hall; it was not yet half past seven. So early in the morning, the house was perfectly still. Since everyone in the Austen house had stayed up late last night, she had small hope that Eliza would be lucid this early in the morning.

No response. Not wanting to wake anyone, Jane gingerly turned the knob and opened the door. "Eliza?" she hissed.

"Jane, go away," Eliza muttered.

Ignoring Eliza's entreaty, Jane slipped inside, closing the door behind her. To her astonishment, Eliza was lying on the bed fully dressed just as Jane had left her the night before. With Marie indisposed, apparently Eliza had decided it was too much trouble to get ready for bed by herself.

"Eliza, wake up!" Jane said, slightly louder this time.

Eliza rolled over and groaned. Slowly she opened an eye, then shaded it from the bright sunlight streaming through the window. "Jane, what are you doing here?" Eliza asked, sitting up. She yawned and stretched her arms above her head. She glanced down at her dress and plucked at the lace at her neck. "Why am I still dressed?"

"Marie never came to you last night?" Jane asked.

Eliza frowned. "Oh, I recall now. I knocked on her door, but she didn't answer. Which is odd; usually she is very reliable."

"It was very late," Jane pointed out. "And she had a terrible headache."

"What time is it now?"

"Early enough that we are the only ones awake. We have to talk seriously, you and I."

"I could never discuss anything in earnest at this hour. My head is fit to break apart," she said, pressing her palms to her skull. Jane couldn't help but notice that even unbrushed and uncurled, Eliza's short hair was flattering.

"Eliza!" Jane cried. Eliza winced, and Jane lowered her voice. "We need to decide what to do about your husband."

Eliza grimaced. "Jean is dead to me."

"Look at me, cousin." Jane waited until she had Eliza's full attention. "The point is that he is not dead. You are a married woman. But judging from your behavior last night, you are enamored of my brother."

Eliza looked away. "Perhaps," she muttered.

"There's no uncertainty about it. You were flirting with him all night long. I saw you in the gazebo with him."

Eliza glared at Jane. "Really, cousin, you should find employment with the War Office; you're becoming quite the little spy. Is no one's privacy safe from you?"

Jane flushed; Eliza's rebuke was fair. "You are not a widow anymore. You have to let Henry go."

"I don't want to." Eliza looked at Jane with eyes that were suddenly clear and tragic. "I think I love him."

"All the more reason for you to behave with more decorum. Henry is an officer, with his living to make in the world. No breath of scandal can touch him. And what about Cassandra and myself? Don't we already have enough marks against us in the matrimonial market that you should also tar us with an adulterous brush?"

Eliza gasped at Jane's blunt speech.

Jane continued, merciless. "Cassandra's fiancé is a very respectable clergyman. He loves her, but he'd think twice about marrying into our family if you persist in misbehaving."

Eliza jumped up and began pacing about the room. "You're blaming *me*? You heard what Jean did. How can you expect me to go to such a monster? Not to mention being exiled to the wilds of America!"

Jane murmured that she had heard Boston was a very civilized city. "It won't be that bad. You and Hastings may like it there."

Eyes blazing, Eliza jabbed a finger at Jane. "Did you notice how he didn't even ask after his own son? Hastings is better off without his father. The only thing the Comte had to offer him was a title—and the Revolution took even that away."

Jane kept a firm grip on her temper. "But the Comte is still very much alive. And all your wishing won't change that. I sympathize with your predicament, but until you have dealt with your husband you absolutely cannot form a new attachment." *Particularly with my brother,* Jane added in her mind.

Returning to the narrow bed, Eliza perched on the edge and rested her chin in her cupped hands. "He only came back for the money."

They were the saddest words Jane had ever heard. And the truest.

Eliza went on tragically. "I'd gladly pay a huge price to rid myself of him."

Jane stared at her, struck by the elegance of Eliza's casual suggestion. "Of course! That is what we shall do."

"I didn't mean it, Jane."

"Didn't you?" Jane insisted. "I propose that we go to him this very morning and demand his price to go away for good."

"Do you think it would work?" Eliza asked doubtfully.

Jane nodded eagerly, warming to her plan. "He would have to swear to stay in America and never return. And of course, he could not use his name."

"And I would be free?" Eliza clasped her hands together. Jane could see she was trembling.

Jane shrugged. "He's been declared dead, so I suppose so."

"Do it!" Eliza hugged Jane. "Go to him and ask him how much my freedom is worth!"

Taken aback, Jane stared. "I cannot do it, Eliza. You should go."

"I cannot. He would try to bully me for the sake of my entire fortune. But you know him for his true cowardly self. And that knowledge will shame him. He will negotiate with you. It must be you, Jane."

Jane was alternately flattered and exasperated. She would enjoy bending the Comte to her will, but it was typical of Eliza to want someone else to clean up her mess.

After a scant moment's hesitation, she agreed. "How much can I offer him?" she asked.

Less than twenty minutes later, Jane tiptoed downstairs. She had little fear of waking anyone as last night's merriment had continued until the small hours of the morning. The gentlemen had been lively indeed, and more than one bottle of port had been emptied.

She slipped her stoutest boots on her feet and wrapped her pelisse about her body.

"Miss Jane? Is that you?" Prudence's voice at her elbow made her jump.

"You startled me!" Jane said sharply, then immediately repented when she saw the stricken look on Prudence's face. The Austens couldn't afford a trained maid, and Prudence was new to a gentleman's house and her duties. "Good morning."

"You're going out?" Prudence asked.

"On Saturday mornings Cassandra cleans the church for the Sunday service," Jane explained. "Since she's not here, it falls to me." To herself she thought that today there was more than dust in the old church. She had to sweep the Comte out of the church and Eliza's life.

"You might want something warm in you before you go out in the snow," Prudence suggested.

Jane thought that was an excellent idea; she would not mind some fortification before facing the Comte again. She and Eliza had left him angry and despairing the night before. Who knew how he would react today?

She followed Prudence into the kitchen. Jacques was there stacking wood by the fireplace under Cook's watchful eye.

"Good morning, Cook, Jacques," Jane said, pouring herself a cup of tea from the teapot on the table.

"Mademoiselle, bon matin." Jacques nodded respectfully.

"Good morning, Miss," Cook said as she rummaged through a drawer full of cooking utensils. "You aren't going to the church in this weather, are you?"

"You say that every Saturday morning in the winter," Jane teased. Cook had worked for the Austens for many years, and Jane was accustomed to her familiar ways. "James is to preach tomorrow, and you know he sneezes if there's too much dust. Someone has to sweep the church."

A large log slipped out of Jacques' hands and crashed to the slate floor.

"Goodness, Jacques, are you all right?" Cook asked.

"Yes, I am fine," he said, his face red. Then he turned to Jane. "Mademoiselle, the way to the church is impassable."

Jane laughed. "I'm not like the Comtesse. Here in the country we are used to walking despite poor conditions."

"I'll accompany you, then," he offered.

"No, thank you," Jane said. "I would rather go alone."

"I insist . . ." he began.

"I said no," Jane said firmly.

"As you wish, mademoiselle," he said, turning to go back outside for more wood.

Cook was muttering under her breath and removing every item from the drawer.

"Is something amiss?" Jane asked. She was very fond of Cook and did not like to see her perturbed.

"My best knife is missing."

"I'm sure it was merely misplaced," Jane said. "Ask Prudence when she comes downstairs." Quickly gulping the last of her tea she went outside, bracing herself against the cold air.

The storm was over. At least a foot of snow had fallen, but now the sky was bright and blue. The whiteness was blinding. Their footprints from the night before were filled in, leaving not a trace of their passage. The powdery snow was almost fun to walk through, and Jane found herself more lighthearted than she expected.

Halfway there she remembered how she had trailed an unsuspecting Eliza the day before. She whirled around suddenly to check for any followers, but no one was in sight.

In just a few minutes she was at the church door. The familiar pointed arch was flanked with stone carvings: a man's head on the left and a woman's on the right. After many years of attending her father's services here, Jane thought of the carvings as old friends. She touched the woman's forehead, borrowing some courage for the encounter ahead.

She knocked loudly; after all, the Comte was nervy and had a pistol. She did not want to startle him.

"It is Jane Austen," she announced, her voice echoing about the clearing. There was no answer within. She pushed open the door. "Hello! Comte?"

The church was cold and appeared to be empty. She quickly made a circuit of the small building but there was no one. The fire had burned out. She held her hand to the ashes, but they were cold.

Hands on her hips, she surveyed the space. The Comte's few belongings were gone. Except for the ashes in the fireplace, there was no trace that he had ever been there.

She went outside and surveyed the area around the church. There was no sign of him. Perhaps he had despaired of winning Eliza back. Perhaps he would just disappear and Eliza could remain a merry widow. But of course how then could she remarry, knowing her husband was still alive?

Resolved to return to the parsonage and tell Eliza that her husband was gone again, Jane pulled the door closed and then realized she had no way to lock it. The Comte must still have the key. It would be no easy matter to get a new key made for the ancient lock.

As she turned to head home, she saw an enormous crow wing its way from the bell tower to the east side of the church, where the graveyard was. In the quiet of the morning, the bird's cawing was unnaturally loud. Soon it was joined by another crow, and then another. "A murder of crows," Jane murmured to herself, shivering a little with foreboding. No doubt a small animal had frozen in the storm and the crows were announcing a free meal to the others.

Curious, she made her way through the deep snow around the corner of the church to the small graveyard. The clearing was punctuated with the tops of gravestones peeking out of the drifts. A crow was perched on the nearest stone, surveying the scene. A dozen yards away more crows were pecking at a long oblong lump hidden under a drift. A streak of crimson marred the perfect whiteness.

Jane stepped slowly closer, dreading what she might see. At the end of the oblong shape, something was sticking up out of the snow. She gasped when she realized it was not another tombstone but the tops of booted feet.

She stood frozen for an instant. There was nothing she wanted to do less than look at whoever was attached to those boots. But she knew her duty. She moved closer.

The boots belonged to a man lying on his back. She couldn't see his face. The hilt of a large knife was stuck in his chest. The crows were digging their beaks into the wound.

"Shoo! Get away! Get away!" she screamed at the crows, waving her arms frantically. She didn't recognize her own voice. The black birds reluctantly lifted off and took up positions in the surrounding trees.

She nerved herself to brush the snow from the figure's face. With a sense of inevitability, she recognized the Comte. His eyes were open, staring unseeingly into the sky. Crystals of ice had formed on his eyelashes and his handsome face was blue.

She stumbled back, her hand to her mouth. It was no use; she bent over and vomited into the snow.

CHAPTER 17

"I never should have mentioned it to you,
if I had not felt the greatest dependence
in the world upon your secrecy."
SENSE AND SENSIBILITY

*W*iping her mouth with the back of her hand, Jane straightened up and breathed deeply. The cold air cut into her lungs, and her eyes stung. Looking anywhere but at the Comte's lifeless body, she scanned the clearing. She felt alone and defenseless. The Comte had been armed with a pistol, but still someone had killed him. Was the murderer still here? What would the killer do to her?

Jane forced herself to look at the Comte again. His face was contorted in a grimace of surprise and pain. She tried to lift his hand but it was frozen, either from death or cold, she didn't know which. There were no footprints breaking up the smooth perfection of the snow, not even the Comte's own. That meant whoever killed him had done it while it was still snowing enough to cover any tracks.

Surely the murderer must be far away by now. When Jane had finally gone to bed at midnight the night before, she had noticed the snow had not yet stopped falling. A shiver went through her body; maybe the killer had been lurking in the woods when Jane and Eliza were still at the church.

She had to get help. Jane headed for the path home, but stopped short when she heard the exultant cawing of the crows. She looked back to see them swooping over the corpse.

She ran at them, windmilling her arms and yelling until they again took flight. She couldn't leave the body unprotected. Jane ran into the church, looking for the blankets she had seen the night before. She raced to the tiny unheated vestry at the back of the church. There were the blankets, neatly folded on a shelf. She grabbed one and a small lacy square of fabric fell to the ground. The handkerchief was trimmed with fine lace and bore an embroidered *E*.

"Eliza, why must you be so careless? You're always . . ."

A memory of Henry tucking Eliza's handkerchief in his waistcoat the night before flew into Jane's mind. She shook her head. Henry had no reason to come to the church.

Stuffing the handkerchief into her pocket, Jane raced back outside, clutching the blanket. She made ready to place it over the Comte's body when she noticed something she hadn't seen before. The knife hilt sticking out of his chest looked familiar.

Steeling herself, because getting closer to that terrible wound was the last thing she wanted to do, she knelt down to examine the knife. There was a deep crack going down the center of the bone handle; Jane would recognize it out of a thousand others. It was Cook's missing knife.

She fell back into the snow, thinking hard. This changed everything. Whoever had killed the Comte de Feuillide had come from her own house.

Henry?

No.

But what about the handkerchief?

No. There were several possible explanations. Eliza had at least a dozen of those handkerchiefs. This one might even have been a keepsake of the Comte's.

Jane told herself that the killer must be someone who had reason to hate him. The killer must be Jacques, she told herself. It had to be.

Jacques had motive. He had a most grievous and righteous grudge against the Comte. Jacques had tried to keep her from coming to the church. And who better than a servant had such access to the Austens' kitchen?

Or maybe it was Marie? More likely Marie had conspired with Jacques. Jane recalled the secretive meeting between them in the garden. What if Marie had discovered the Comte was still alive—after all, Eliza was not the most discreet!—and told her brother-in-law?

Jane started to push herself up from the ground and her hand struck something soft. She flinched. Surely it couldn't be more awful than a dead body.

Jane felt gingerly about in the snow and pulled out a black hat. She remembered how the Comte had tilted the hat to hide his face. That was puzzling. How could the hat accumulate a foot of snow but the Comte's body only a few inches?

Jane stood up and shook the snow from her skirts. There were too many questions. She needed to talk to someone. Tom Lefroy's face popped into her mind but she rejected him out of hand. She needed someone she could trust absolutely. Someone strong, preferably armed, who would return with her to the church and deal with the body.

She should probably get James; in their father's absence he was in charge of the church. The War Office suspected

Eliza was spying for the French—if they found out the Comte was not dead, that would confirm their suspicions. But James saw everything as black and white, true and false. Subtlety, and perhaps a certain degree of moral flexibility, were required to preserve Eliza's reputation. Jane needed help, but from someone who would put Eliza's interests first. Henry loved Eliza; he was the one to fetch.

She quickly placed the blanket over the Comte's body, being sure to cover his head. She didn't want to think about the crows pecking away at his eyes. She hurried home.

As she approached, she saw movement in the garden and darted behind a tree to watch.

Jacques was chopping more wood. He lifted the ax above his head and brought the blade down with enough force to drive it clear through a thick log. Jane shivered. He was strong enough to stab the Comte, that was certain.

As quietly as she could, she opened the door and slipped inside. Without troubling to take off her coat, she hurried upstairs. "Henry!" she whispered. "Open the door! Henry!"

She heard him stumbling about the room, then a crack and a muffled curse. The door opened a few inches. Henry, unshaven and definitely the worse for a night of hard drinking, peered out at her. He was still wearing his trousers from last night, and his shirt hung loose. "Jane?" he asked, not concealing his irritation. "Why are you knocking at this ungodly hour?"

"Keep your voice down," Jane whispered. "I need you at the church."

He glared at her. "If you think I'm going to help you clean, you're mad."

"It's not that." She hesitated. Was there an easy way to say what she had to say? She pushed into his room and whispered, "Henry, there's a dead body there."

His forehead creased in confusion. "Is there a funeral today?"

"Not that kind of body." She watched carefully to see if his face might betray him. "Someone's been killed," she finally said. She couldn't say more in the house. And when Henry saw that knife, he would understand her urgency.

"Who?"

"I can't discuss it here," she said. "But I need your help. Now."

Something in her expression must have convinced him she was in earnest, because he nodded. "I'll be just a moment," he said, starting to close the door.

"Bring your pistol," she hissed.

He froze and stared at her. Slowly he nodded and shut the door. She leaned against the wall and took a deep breath. She wasn't alone any longer.

"Good morning, Jane."

Jane spun around. Tom stood there. Like Henry, he still wore last night's clothes, but his curly hair was at least partially tamed and his white shirt was neatly tucked in.

Jane forced her countenance into a neutral smile. "Why, good morning, Tom."

Henry opened his door and stepped out. He looked relieved when he saw Tom. "Lefroy! Just the fellow!" he exclaimed. "My sister needs our help, and a lawyer might be required."

"But . . ." Jane started faintly.

"I've told you before that I am at your service," Tom said with a short bow.

Jane grimaced, but there was nothing she could do without revealing what she knew. So the threesome hurried outside and down the snowy path.

Both Henry and Tom had the air of dressing hastily, their greatcoats misbuttoned and their scarves tied clumsily about their necks. Tom seemed to be enjoying the novelty. "What, may I inquire, could require legal services so early on a Saturday morning?"

"Jane has found a body."

Tom pulled up. "What?"

Jane waved her arms. "Come on," she said. "It'll be far faster to simply show the two of you."

Only a few minutes passed before Jane led them to the graveyard and the shrouded body. Tom and Henry, suddenly sobered, stared down. No one wanted to remove the blanket.

"Who is it?" Henry asked impatiently.

Her eyes fixed on Henry's face, Jane said quietly, "It is the Comte de Feuillide."

Henry's face paled. "Eliza's husband?"

"But I thought he was guillotined," Tom said, confused.

"We all did. Apparently, he managed to keep his head," Jane confirmed. "He's been in hiding." She reached down and lifted the blanket. Tom looked green. Henry was made of sterner stuff, but his shock was plain to see.

"That is Jean," Henry said. Jane dropped the blanket. Henry's face was impassive. Jane could guess, however, in what turmoil his thoughts must be. He had spent a summer with the Comte in France a few years ago and had thought of him as a friend. He had mourned when the Comte was killed. And yet now he coveted the Comte's wife.

"How did he escape the guillotine?" Tom asked.

"More importantly, did Eliza know he was still alive?" Henry's voice was full of hurt. Jane didn't blame him. Eliza had not been acting like a woman who knew her husband was living.

"She only found out at the ball," she said.

"So last night . . ."

"She had decided to break with him. I'm sure she would have told you soon." Jane placed her hand on his arm for comfort. She couldn't help but notice that Henry's coat was sopping wet, and the smell of damp wool filled her nose. But the day was clear and sunny. He had been in his shirtsleeves the night before in the gazebo. When did he wear his coat in the snow?

Her heart constricted, and it hurt to breathe.

Not Henry.

But he was so in love with Eliza. What wouldn't he have done to keep her? And that handkerchief! Did it place him at the church last night? She couldn't take another step without finding out for sure.

"Henry, do you have her handkerchief?" She didn't need to specify whose handkerchief she meant.

"From last night? Of course I do," he said. His hand went to his waist. "Why do you ask?"

Tom, suddenly alert, was watching Jane's face with speculation. "If I had to guess, Henry old boy, your sister found a similar handkerchief at the scene and wants to make sure you didn't drop it."

Henry straightened up and took a step back. "Jane, is that true? You think I would have done this?"

"Just show me the handkerchief."

Henry pressed his lips into a thin line as he reached inside his coat and pulled out the lacy square. Holding it out to her, he said, "Here."

Just to be sure, she had to ask him. "Henry, why is your coat wet?"

Tom turned away from the scene before him. A gentleman should avoid watching another gentleman be humiliated by his younger sister.

"I went out last night to get some air," Henry said. "I was only out for ten minutes or so. Tom, do you remember? After my brother won that big hand, after the ladies went to bed. We'd had too much port, and I went outside to clear my head. The snow was coming down hard." He glared at his sister. "Are you satisfied now?"

Jane glanced at Tom, who nodded almost imperceptibly.

"Henry, I'm sorry, but you see I had to ask," Jane said. "The Comte stood between you and your heart's desire. I needed to be sure that no one could say you killed him."

"Based on a handkerchief and a kiss in the garden?" Henry asked scornfully.

Tom, his eyes fixed on Jane's face, said, "There's something else, isn't there."

"Look at the knife," Jane said.

Tom and Henry squatted down to look more closely at the Comte's body.

"It's an ordinary kitchen knife," Tom said.

Henry caught his breath. "No. It's not."

"It's Cook's favorite," Jane said. "The weapon used to kill the Comte came from our house."

"I'm sure there is a logical explanation," Tom said, trying to be reassuring. "The magistrate will get to the bottom of this."

Jane and Henry exchanged anxious looks. "Our magistrate is Mr. Bigg-Wither," Jane said slowly. "He'll never travel in the snow."

"That idiot from the dance?" Tom asked. "He'll be of no help at all. What about a constable? There must be one in Deane."

"Don't be so quick to call in the law, Tom," Henry cautioned, getting to his feet. "The situation is more complicated than you know."

Jane nodded, knowing that Henry was thinking about the cloud of suspicion surrounding Eliza.

"The law is the law," Tom said. "If you find a body, you summon the magistrate or a constable as soon as you can."

"But this man has been dead for over a year," Henry said.

"Very clever, Henry," Tom said. "But a body is still a body."

"A woman's reputation is at stake," Henry said. "Once the authorities are involved, we have no discretion."

"The Comtesse?" Tom asked. "Who could attach any blame to her? She thought her husband was dead."

"But she is already suspect," Jane said slowly. "Our brother Edward was charged by the War Office to watch her for any treasonous activities. They look for sedition everywhere, and they will never believe that she didn't know the truth. And by extension, the reputation of all the Austens will be tarnished."

"Surely you exaggerate?" Tom said.

"The country is at war, Tom," Henry said. "We dare not make this public without talking to the War Office."

A stubborn expression on his face, Tom shook his head. "We have no choice. I'm to be a member of the bar. Regardless of the consequences, you must follow the rules."

"Please help us," Jane entreated. She rather liked that the insouciant Tom had some principles, but those principles were a little awkward at the moment. "What exactly does the law say we are obligated to do?"

Tom looked puzzled by the question. "You must report a crime within a reasonable amount of time."

"Ah." Jane beamed. "There's been a deep snowfall. It's difficult to get word to anyone. So if we delayed reporting it for say, forty-eight hours, no one could fault us."

"How does a delay help you?" Tom asked.

"If we have a little time, perhaps we can solve this crime ourselves," she answered, feeling suddenly more optimistic. "There need not be any publicity if the magistrate already knows who did it."

"I cannot be a party to the obstruction of justice." Tom's eyes narrowed as he considered. Finally he said, "But on the other hand, the roads are terrible. It might well be that they won't be clear until tomorrow."

"Thank you, Tom," Jane said.

"But you must tell the magistrate everything. I'll insist on that. I have my career to think of."

"Agreed!" Jane said, her voice quickening with excitement.

"Not only is the victim related to you and the scene of the crime intimately connected with your family, but the weapon comes from the Austen kitchen." Tom slowly stood. "I cannot help but wonder how much of this caution is because the crime strikes so close to home."

Henry was trying to catch Jane's eye. He clearly regretted his impulsive invitation for Tom to join them. She knew her brother was thinking the same thing she was: What if someone they cared about was the killer? Would Tom be on their side—or the side of justice?

Jane reached out and took Tom's hand. "I swear to you that I have no direct knowledge of who killed the Comte de Feuillide."

"Nor do I," Henry vowed.

Tom held onto Jane's hand a few moments longer than were needed. "I trust you."

"Thank you. But in the meantime, we can't leave this poor man here," Jane said. "It's not dignified." Her eyes darted to the trees on the edge of the clearing. "There are crows." She had to clear her throat.

Tom and Henry grimaced.

"We'll have to hide the body for now," Henry said practically.

"We can take him into the vestry," Jane said. "It's not heated and it is very private."

"You can't hide the body forever," Tom warned.

"We have one day," Jane said. "Anyway, that's when James will prepare for his sermon tomorrow. He's not very observant, but even he would notice a body in the vestry."

As they lifted the Comte's body, Jane could see the perfect shape of his form left in the snow. To her surprise, there was a large pool of frozen blood where his back had lain.

"Wait!" she called after Tom and Henry. "Let me see his back."

"Jane, he's heavy," her brother grunted.

"Can't it wait until we're inside?" Tom asked.

"It will only take a moment," Jane promised.

Henry and Tom twisted the body. "Look!" she said, pointing to a spot just beneath the Comte's ribs. "He was stabbed in the back twice. These two cuts are shallower but just as deadly. They must have struck the heart."

"Who would stab him in the back and then the front?" Henry asked.

"Maybe he was already dead," Tom suggested.

"What do you mean?" Jane asked.

"There's hardly any blood from the knife wound in his chest, yet an inordinate quantity seems to have drained from his back. Maybe he was already dead when he was stabbed in the chest?"

"Maybe the knife from our kitchen wasn't the one that killed him," Jane said excitedly.

"Then why is it here?" Henry asked. "Just to cast suspicion on our house?"

"If that was the reason, the knife fulfilled its purpose admirably," Jane said. "I even suspected you, dear Henry."

Jane ran ahead of them to open the vestry door. Her mind was full of questions. Chief among them was why would anyone stab a dead man? And did the killer mean to incriminate her own family?

CHAPTER 18

*"Do not consider me now as an elegant female
intending to plague you, but as a rational
creature speaking the truth from her heart."*
PRIDE AND PREJUDICE

After the three of them deposited the body on a bench in the dark vestry, Jane adjusted the blanket to hide the Comte's terrible face.

Tom shivered. "It feels colder in here than it does outside," he said.

"There's no sunlight in here," Jane said.

"Let me take you home, Jane," Tom said. "Whether you admit it or not, this has been a shock for you."

"Yes, sister, stop being so brave," Henry said.

Hugging herself to keep warm, Jane shook her head. "Not yet," she said. "There are too many unanswered questions." As she stared down at the body, a glint of gold caught her eye. "What is that?" She started to reach for it, but Tom pulled her away.

"I'll do it," Henry said. Grimacing, he pried open the Comte's fingers. Jane averted her eyes. "It's a cross," he said. "He was Catholic; he must have clutched it for comfort as he was dying."

Tom frowned; Jane agreed it was puzzling. "If he was stabbed in the back," Jane mused, "would he have had time to take his necklace off and pray?"

"That wound from the back was what killed him," Tom agreed. "It must have pierced his heart."

"How would you know?" Jane asked.

"I wasn't always a lawyer. I grew up on a farm," he said simply. "I've butchered my share of animals."

"Perhaps he tore it off the killer's neck," Jane said.

"Give it to me," Jane said, holding out her hand to Henry. She held it up to the tiny window of leaded glass. One of the links of the chain was broken. Dangling from the chain was a lovely ornate gold cross. "This looks familiar. I'll ask Eliza if she recognizes it."

"You don't think . . ." Henry couldn't finish his sentence.

"Eliza's not Catholic, and I've never seen her wear this. But she will know if it was the Comte's." A stray recollection teased the corner of her mind until she remembered. "I think I've seen something like it around the neck of her maid, Marie."

"Her maid?" Tom asked. "Why would she kill the Comte?"

"Her husband was the Comte's valet," Jane explained.

"The valet who was supposed to have died with the Comte?" Henry asked.

"Will someone please tell me how is it that the Comte de Feuillide survived the guillotine?" Tom asked crossly.

Jane glanced at the body. "Let's go outside, where the air is not tainted with death."

When they reached the door, Jane said, "Henry, we have to lock the church."

"Fine," he said. "Give me the key."

"I don't have it." She glanced back toward the vestry. "I think the Comte had it last."

"Then that's where it will stay," Henry said. "I'm not searching the pockets of a corpse."

"We cannot leave the church open to anyone who might pass by," Jane argued. "We just left a body there!"

With a sigh, Tom said, "You two are worse than my little brothers and sisters! I'll look." A few minutes later, a pale-faced Tom rejoined them and silently gave Jane the key. She carefully locked the door and stowed the key away in her pocket.

"It's time you told us what you know," Tom said.

"It's a long story; you might as well sit," she said, gesturing to a stone bench outside the church.

"Jane, it's freezing," Henry complained.

"Sit," she ordered. Obediently, Henry and Tom brushed off the snow and sat down.

Jane told them everything, from overhearing Edward's plan to spy on Eliza to the real reason Eliza had swooned at the ball. She ended her story with the events from the night before. Tom nodded throughout, as though sorting the details into neat dockets in his mind. Henry grew progressively more upset.

"When I came out this morning to try to negotiate with the Comte, he was dead," Jane finished.

"Are you all right, Jane?" Tom asked. "That must have been terrible for you."

"Jane is tough," Henry said. "She can take care of herself. But for my poor Eliza to suffer so!"

"Yes, Henry," Jane said without sympathy. "Poor Eliza. We know. But what about Jacques and Marie? They've suffered, too. René was Marie's husband and Jacques' brother. They lost him because of the Comte's selfishness."

Tom was deep in thought. Finally he said, "The Comte is morally guilty of murder, if not legally. But no one deserves to be murdered. He should have faced a trial."

"So you don't think that whoever killed the Comte might be justified?" Jane asked, curious to hear his answer.

"Murder is murder," Tom said. "There can be no excuse for stabbing a man in the back. I'm sure the magistrate will agree."

Henry and Jane exchanged worried glances. "It would be better if we find out who did it first," Jane said.

Henry nodded his fervent agreement. "How do we start?" he asked.

"I've not yet conducted a criminal trial," Tom said, "but I've observed several. The Crown's prosecutor always focuses on three elements of the crime: motive, opportunity, and means. Let's begin with the first. *Cui bono*?" Looking at Jane, he added, "That is Latin for 'Who benefits?'"

Henry guffawed. "No need to translate for Jane. She was the best of Father's students. I daresay her Latin is better than mine."

"Not a difficult fence to clear," Jane said, giving both of them a withering look.

"Yes, let's take the maid first," Henry said. "We've found a piece of jewelry that Jane believes belongs to her. The Comte was responsible for her husband's death."

Tom nodded thoughtfully. "Revenge is as good a motive as any."

"Would Marie have the strength to stab her employer in the back?" Jane asked doubtfully.

"Who knows what she might have done in the grip of a temper?" Henry said.

"Even in a paroxysm of rage, is she strong enough?" Tom asked. "That knife is lodged in the Comte's chest bone. A powerful hand struck that blow."

"And when she spoke of her husband, it was with affection, not any stronger emotion," Jane recalled.

"Perhaps there is another explanation for the necklace," Tom said.

"Eliza may know," Jane agreed.

Tom cleared his throat. "Speaking of your cousin . . ."

Henry turned his head to watch Tom's face. "What about her?"

"Are we certain that the Comtesse did not kill her husband?"

"That is a base accusation! Take it back!" Henry leapt to his feet, fists at the ready. Tom remained seated, but poised to defend himself.

"Henry, sit down!" Jane said sharply. "Tom's question is fair, and you are not doing Eliza any favors by blindly defending her." After all, Jane thought, Eliza had threatened her husband the night before—a fact Jane had not mentioned to Henry and Tom. She caught Tom's eye. "Prove your case, Mr. Lefroy, if you can."

Watching Henry warily, Tom said, "Henry, my friend, I did not mean any disrespect. But the Comtesse has an overwhelming motive. The Comte abandoned her and their son. And now he returns, without so much as a by-your-leave, and wants her to give up everything she holds dear and go to America. He threatened to take her son. As her husband, legally he has the right. She would be powerless to stop him."

Henry glowered but stayed silent.

"And, pardon me, Henry," Tom said, staring past him into the clearing, "but the lady is in love with a man who is not her husband. How is her lot not improved by his death?"

Tom's summary struck Jane with a hammer's force. She was equally admiring of his logic and appalled by it. He went on, inexorable. "She had opportunity. She was one of the few who knew where he was."

"I knew, too," Jane said.

He smiled tentatively at her. "I exclude you from our consideration because you have no reason to kill him, and if you did, you would not be foolish enough to tell us. The Comtesse knew where to find him. And last night most of us were too indisposed and tired to note her whereabouts."

"I was watching her the whole time," Henry declared.

"Even after she retired for the night?" Tom asked, splotches of color appearing on his fair cheeks.

Henry was silent. "Don't be so chivalrous, Henry," Jane said impatiently. "Can you account for Eliza's whereabouts all night or not?"

"No, of course not. And I resent the implication, on Eliza's behalf and my own," Henry muttered. "But that doesn't mean that she did anything wrong."

"No, it doesn't," Jane agreed. "And the snow last night would have made the path here very difficult. She's not a strong walker."

"Still, we have motive and opportunity. Now as to means," Tom said. "She had access to the knife."

"But she's tiny," Jane said. "There is no way she could inflict any of those wounds, even the shallower ones. And my cousin is no fool. Why leave a knife in the body that could be traced back to our house?"

"Maybe it was the only knife she could find," Tom countered. "And don't forget the handkerchief. It proves she was here."

"We know she was here," Jane countered. "I was here with her. Besides, anyone could have dropped it in the church." She pulled out the handkerchief again. "Look at the darning on the corner. Eliza would never carry such a thing. She would have discarded it immediately. Anyone from here to London might have picked it up."

Tom pursed his lips as though he wanted to argue with her. Jane held up a hand. "Eliza is family and my dear friend, so I know you don't trust our faith in her. But I have a vivid imagination. Try as I might, I cannot see her creeping out of the house in the middle of a storm, luring her husband out in the snow, and stabbing him twice in the back and then again in his chest. I honestly do not believe that she did it."

"Thank you, Jane," Henry said, wiping his brow. He took his place on the bench, his fingers drumming on his knees.

Tom gazed at her with admiration. "Jane, would you take it amiss if I told you that your powers of deduction are as logical as any man's?"

"I would say you do not know enough women," Jane retorted.

"Look, Tom, you've made her blush!" Henry crowed. "Hardly anyone has the power to do that." His delight in teasing his sister trumped, for an instant, the gravity of the situation.

"Don't talk nonsense," Jane said severely. "Tom, if we are agreed that we can exclude Eliza . . ."

"For now," he said cautiously.

"Then we must consider other possibilities," Jane finished.

"Who do you believe might have done the deed?" Tom asked.

Without pausing, she said, "Jacques, Eliza's coachman."

"That insolent fellow who wouldn't give you the mail?" Tom asked.

She nodded and explained her suspicions of Jacques. "So you see, he is most likely spying on his mistress either for the French regime or for the English—who knows? He has reason to hate the Comte, who was responsible for the death of his brother. He tried to keep me from coming here this morning. And he is a big man, certainly strong enough to inflict the wounds we saw."

"What about the chain?" Tom asked.

"I don't know," Jane admitted. "I've never noticed whether Jacques wore one. But we mustn't assume that the owner of the necklace is the killer. It might have belonged to the Comte. Although, if the killer did wear it, there may be marks around his or her neck from where the necklace was ripped away. Or there may be an entirely innocent explanation."

"We should watch Jacques carefully," Henry said eagerly. "He might try to flee. After all, he has Eliza's carriage."

"We don't have an unassailable case yet," Tom said, "but there is definitely enough to suspect him. It would be best if he were still here to talk to the magistrate."

"The two of you must make sure he doesn't run," Jane said. "And I will find out more about this necklace." She ran the chain through her fingers, feeling the cold metal grow warmer. "I have to tell Eliza what's happened."

"Jane, I'd prefer to tell her," Henry said.

"No!" Jane and Tom cried in unison.

"You mustn't talk to Eliza before I do," Jane said.

"Why not?" Henry was as petulant as a little boy.

"It is not proper for you, of all people, to tell her that her husband is dead."

Henry's crestfallen expression reminded Jane of how he used to look when their mother forbade him some treat.

"Even though I think she is innocent," Jane said, "she may have knowledge that will help us." Unspoken was Jane's conviction that Eliza could mislead Henry and he would never think to challenge her. "And then I'll talk to Marie."

"Very well. I'll guard Jacques," Henry said. "Tom, you'll watch over Jane?"

"I don't need watching over!" Jane exclaimed.

"Jane, there's a murderer loose," Tom said. "The last thing I . . . we want is for you to be the next victim. Henry, I'll take care of her."

"Do you want to borrow my pistol?" Henry asked.

"That's not necessary!" Jane cried.

Tom held up his hands. "You'll need it more than I," he said hastily. "Jacques is more likely to give you trouble."

"As far as we know, he's not armed," Henry protested. "But the ladies, they are the more dangerous sex by far!"

"Enough!" Jane snapped. "No one is armed except my idiot brother." Even as she said it, she wondered if it were true. The Comte had had a pistol. Tom hadn't found it on his body; he would have said so. Where was it? And where were his belongings? She remembered seeing his leather satchel near the fire the night before. Perhaps the gun had been taken away by the murderer.

She started to tell the others, but was interrupted by Henry. "We've been gone long enough. Let's go home," he said. "Mother hates to wait breakfast for us. I'm starved."

Tom agreed. "We mustn't rouse anyone's suspicions. It will be easier if no one knows what we are about."

Jane, feeling the chill in her feet and the emptiness in her stomach, was amenable. She would tell them about the pistol later.

Henry set off ahead of Jane and Tom, arms swinging. His tousled blond hair caught the sun. Jane envied him his easy ability to shake off tragedy.

"Life is easy for people like Henry," Tom said.

Jane was startled; his words echoed her thoughts exactly. "What do you mean?"

Tom shrugged. "A younger son. No expectations. He can think only of himself and no one will think any less of him."

"He's worried about Eliza," Jane pointed out.

"And that's not selfish?" Tom asked.

"Eliza is the first thing his charm might not secure for him," Jane said. "But he perseveres nonetheless. I think his feelings are genuine. However, you are right; he is the most lighthearted of all my brothers."

"He is certainly more entertaining than James!"

They both laughed, and it was as if a heavy weight had been lifted from her shoulders.

"James is not so bad," Jane said. "But he is the oldest and feels the responsibility of that."

"I sympathize," Tom said. "I'm the oldest son in a large family, too."

"But you aren't as poor as we are!" Jane said, her eyes fixed on the ground. If Tom didn't already know that she had no fortune, he did now. He was silent, and she let her gaze wander to see his face.

"My father was even poorer," Tom said. "He was an ensign in the army. His only patron was his uncle, Judge Langlois. Father fell in love with the daughter of an impoverished local squire. But he knew my great-uncle wouldn't approve of such an improvident match."

"What did he do?" Jane asked, working hard to keep her tone casual.

"He married her, but kept it secret."

Jane's laugh was more a snort. "How long could that stratagem succeed?"

"The judge lives in London and refused to visit Ireland. Father was certain that if he presented his uncle with an heir, then all would be forgiven."

"And you are the heir in question?" Jane asked, smiling.

"Only after five sisters," he said.

"Five! Every new girl dashing your family's prospects!" She could not help laughing at the idea.

Tom shrugged. "Happily I was born. But I am at the mercy of the same pigheadedness. All my hopes rest on my great-uncle's favor."

Jane didn't answer. She was lost in thought. Her fingers tingled, longing for a pen. What possibilities there were in Tom's story! A family desperate for a son. Perhaps the property is entailed and only a male relative can inherit. But daughter after daughter is born. Their only hope is to marry well. But how can five girls all manage to find husbands? The Austens couldn't manage two!

"Jane?" Tom's voice interrupted her plotting.

She came back to herself. "I'm sorry."

"I thought you were lost to me; your thoughts were so far away."

"Not at all. I'm grateful. You've given me the seed of a story. Who knows what it will grow into?"

He looked puzzled. "I cannot imagine what kind of tale you could spin from my dull family, but I look forward to seeing it."

As they walked, they kept to the path their footsteps had trod on the way to the church. The sun was bright but not warm, for which Jane was grateful. The longer the road was impassable, the more time she had to think of a way to protect Eliza and the Austen name. She sighed at the size of the task before her.

The parsonage was in sight, windows gleaming. "Your home is charming," Tom said.

"It's drafty and dreadfully plain," Jane retorted.

"The warmth of your family's hospitality more than compensates for the chill."

"You are very gallant," Jane said. Stopping on the doorstep, she turned to Tom. "When I first met you, I never would have thought that we could be friends."

"When we first met, I was a churlish idiot. My only redeeming feature is that I can learn from my mistakes." He reached out and took her hand. "I am honored to be your friend. Perhaps more than friends."

Jane felt warmth spread from his hand to hers. She squeezed his hand ever so slightly and for a moment forgot about Eliza, the dead Comte, and all their troubles.

CHAPTER 19

*I will venture to say that my
investigations and decisions are not usually
influenced by my hopes or fears.*
PRIDE AND PREJUDICE

"*J*ane, there you are!" A voice from above drew their eyes upward. Eliza's worried face poked out of a half-open window. Unobtrusively, Jane withdrew her hand from Tom's. "I've been waiting and waiting. Tell me everything!"

"I'll come in a moment," Jane promised. Eliza nodded and closed the window.

"Should I come with you when you talk to the Comtesse?" Tom asked.

"I don't think so," Jane said. "She is more likely to confide in me if we are alone."

"Very well. I'll wait downstairs."

Jane tried to tell him that it was unnecessary, but he insisted, reminding her there was a killer about. "If you insist," she said. "Do as you like." She slipped inside.

Eliza was waiting at the top of the stairs. She pulled Jane into her bedroom and closed the door. They were alone. "What did he say?" Eliza asked. "Will he take our offer? Is Hastings safe?"

"Not precisely," Jane said, trying to find the words to tell Eliza that she was a widow. Again.

"Even knowing that I don't want to go to America, he insists that I go with him?" Eliza wailed. "I think I hate him."

"Don't say that," Jane said, remembering the Comte's eyes, glassy in death, staring up at the sky.

"But I do, Jane! I wish he were still dead!"

Jane couldn't let Eliza keep talking as though the Comte was still alive. "Eliza, he *is* dead," she blurted.

Eliza blinked. "What do you mean?"

"I found him lying dead in the snow."

"Dead?" Eliza repeated slowly as if trying to take it in. She sank into her chair.

"Murdered."

Her blue eyes widened. "Murdered?" Jane nodded.

Eliza gripped Jane's hand tightly. "It's an answer to my prayers," she whispered. "Now I can marry Henry. And Hastings and I will stay in England."

Suddenly she looked worried. "Will everyone have to know? Will Henry have to find out that Jean was still alive?"

Jane snatched back her hand. "Of course people will know. Bodies have a way of being noticed. Besides, Henry is already aware of the whole story."

"You told him? Jane, how could you?" Eliza leapt to her feet and began pacing angrily about the room. She picked up a silk scarf and twisted it between her hands. "Does he blame me?"

"He understands," Jane assured her. "And we'll do our best to keep this as quiet as we can, for your sake."

"And yours," Eliza said shrewdly.

Jane pulled the chain and cross from her pocket. "Do you recognize this?"

Eliza squinted until she took the necklace to the window and held it up to the light. "Oh, yes, I know this! Ten years ago Jean went to Rome. He met the pope. He had these necklaces blessed as gifts for his servants. Where did you find this?"

"Did he keep one for himself?" Jane asked, ignoring Eliza's question.

Eliza's brow furrowed in thought. "Yes," she said finally. "But I think Hastings has it now."

"Which servants?"

"Jacques and his brother were each given one."

"Not Marie?"

"No. She hadn't come to work for us yet. But I think she might have René's necklace. I've seen her wear it." Eliza's face was full of questions. "Why are you asking about an old necklace? Where did you find it?"

"We found it clutched in the Comte's hand," Jane explained.

Eliza's hand went to the hollow at the base of her throat. "Do you think one of my servants killed him? No, Jane, it's impossible. They were devoted to Jean."

"Do you include Jacques in that number?"

"Until yesterday, I would have said he was absolutely loyal. But that was before I knew what Jean did to Jacques' brother."

"He has a strong motive," Jane agreed.

"How could he know what Jean had done? I didn't know until last night and I didn't tell anyone."

Jane admitted the truth of that. "What about Marie?"

Eliza shook her head decisively. "Marie would never harm Jean. She owed him everything."

"But his actions led to her husband's death," Jane pointed out.

"Nonsense. Marie was happy enough with René, but it was no love match. Marie was a girl on Jean's estate who got into trouble. She was with child and had no husband." She shrugged as if to say "these things happen."

"Who was the father?"

Eliza shrugged. "Someone on the estate; I never knew. Jean arranged for her to marry René. So she was grateful to Jean for safeguarding her reputation and ensuring her son was provided for."

Jane added these facts to the ones she already had. It didn't seem as though Marie would have a reason to kill the Comte.

Eliza went on. "Besides, Marie, like Jacques, had no way of knowing what my husband had done."

"But unlike Jacques, she is with you all the time. Could you have let slip anything about Jean being alive?"

Eliza couldn't meet Jane's eyes.

"Eliza?" Jane demanded. "What aren't you telling me?"

"I knew it was a secret about Jean. But I needed my warm clothes!" Eliza finally burst out. "I told her that I had to go to the church yesterday and that she should lay out my coat and gloves. I might have mentioned Jean." She frowned. "I don't really remember. I was in a state."

"Marie could have told Jacques," Jane pointed out. "He's intelligent and could have figured out how Jean survived the guillotine."

Jane slipped her hand into her pocket and fingered the other bit of evidence, the handkerchief. After a moment's reflection, she decided that Eliza had so many such bits of linen, there was no point in asking her about it. "Can you fetch Marie?" she asked finally.

Eliza lifted her eyebrows. "Why?"

"Don't worry. I just want to ask her to show me something."

"Very well," Eliza said reluctantly. "It's very aggravating to have to go find my servants. Jane, this house needs bells."

"Eliza, please?"

Eliza hurried out of the room. A few minutes later she returned with Marie in tow.

"Hello, Marie," Jane said. Surreptitiously she examined Marie's throat. The maid still wore two chains round her neck.

Marie bobbed a curtsy. "Mademoiselle."

"Are you feeling better?" Jane asked. "Last night you were indisposed."

"Much better," Marie said.

"Is that why you didn't come to me last night?" Eliza asked.

"I took some laudanum," Marie said. "But I must have taken too much because I slept through the whole night and neglected my duties. Je suis désolée."

There was an awkward silence as Eliza and Marie waited for Jane to speak.

"Marie, may I see your necklaces?" Jane asked.

Marie's attention suddenly sharpened. "May I ask why, mademoiselle?"

"No," Jane answered.

Marie unfastened her necklaces and laid them on the chest near the door. One held the locket containing her son's picture, and the other looked very much like the chain and cross in Jane's pocket.

Jane didn't need both, but she didn't want to draw any more attention to the cross than she had to. Jane's fingers twitched in her eagerness to examine the necklaces. "Thank you, Marie. I'll return them to you presently."

Eliza understood that Jane wanted Marie to go. "You may leave us now," she said. Marie left reluctantly, her eyes fixed on her jewelry.

Once the door had closed, Jane hurried to the chest, pulling the cross from her pocket. She compared it to the one that was still warm from Marie's skin. They were identical, down to the intricately worked chain. "She didn't lose her necklace at the church," she announced.

Eliza breathed a sigh of relief. "Thank goodness. I wouldn't know what to do without her."

"But the evidence is mounting against Jacques," Jane reminded her. She carefully placed the cross and the locket in her skirt pocket. She would return them to Marie herself later.

The porcelain clock that Eliza always traveled with chimed the ten o'clock hour. "It's time for breakfast," Jane said. "Are you coming down?" Since Eliza was still wearing a charming dressing gown, Jane doubted it.

Eliza sat down at the vanity table and peered at the battered mirror. The spots on the glass marred her reflection. "I look terrible," she said, taking a hairbrush to her short curls. "Henry cannot see me until I've done something about my face."

Jane marveled that Eliza could worry about her appearance when she had just learned that her husband had been murdered. But on the other hand, her life with the Comte had not been happy. Eliza, for all her faults, was no hypocrite.

She didn't see his body, Jane thought. If Eliza had seen what Jane had seen, she would not be so carefree.

"Can you send Prudence up with some tea? I'm famished," Eliza said over her shoulder as Jane left the room.

Downstairs the breakfast table was empty save for James and Tom. Mrs. Austen was not feeling well.

"Where is Henry?" Jane asked, hoping that he was outside watching Jacques.

"He rode into Basingstoke," James said. "I don't know what errand he had that was so important that he had to go in this snow, but he left a few minutes past on horseback."

"Alone?" Jane asked. "Are the roads safe?"

His mouth full of toast, James shook his head. Tom took it upon himself to explain. "Henry had Jacques harness a plow horse to a wagon, and Jacques is accompanying him. They'll get through."

"Ah," Jane said. She could guess why Henry had gone to Basingstoke. It was the quickest way to get a message to Edward. She had no doubt that Henry had his orders to send word of anything untoward. Even Edward and his spying friends would be surprised by this news!

Jane was of two minds about Edward and his precious War Office. On the one hand, Jane could use his help if they were to keep the murder quiet, but it might make the War Office even more suspicious of Eliza. They might insist that a magistrate be called sooner rather than later.

She ate quickly and then excused herself with the pretense that she needed to write. As she hoped, Tom soon joined her by the fire. "Don't worry about Henry," he said. "He has his pistol, and Jacques has no idea that we suspect him."

"I'm not worried," Jane lied. "My brother can take care of himself, and it is a clever way to make his report to his superiors and still keep an eye on Jacques."

"Superiors?" Tom asked.

"I forgot," Jane snapped. "You don't know that Henry was sent here to watch Eliza."

"Who sent him?"

"My brother Edward is involved with the War Office. He told Henry to come here."

Tom shook his head in wonder. "I thought the Austens were just a simple country family with a charming daughter. But there are circles within circles of intrigue."

Jane rocked with laughter. "I assure you, under normal circumstances we are as dull as ditch-water. But Eliza brings drama with her wherever she goes." She heard the envy in her voice.

"You shouldn't wish for excitement," Tom said, placing his hand over hers. "Better to hope for a quiet marriage and a family and a pleasant life. My parents have that, and they are very happy."

"That's true," she agreed. She glanced down at his hand. It was a gentleman's hand, soft from an academic life. But Jane could feel old calluses on his palms from his time on the farm. "My parents are content, too. If only they didn't worry so about finances."

"I'm the eldest son of twelve," Tom said with a chuckle. "Worrying about money comes as naturally to me as breathing."

"But now you have a wealthy patron and a career to follow," Jane said. "How I envy men the ability to earn their own money."

"Perhaps one day you can make a tidy sum with your novels," he suggested.

Jane lifted her eyebrows. With the exception of her own family, most men disapproved of women writers. "Perhaps someday," she said wistfully. "But even my stories cannot intrigue me as much as the adventure we are in the midst of now."

Tom put a finger to his lips. He went to the door and peered out. Satisfied that they were alone, he closed the door and returned. "What did your cousin say?"

"She took the news remarkably well," Jane said, unable to keep the censure out of her voice.

"Did you expect her to be prostrated with grief?" Tom asked logically. "Her life is immeasurably easier if he stays dead."

Reluctantly, Jane agreed. "Eliza recognized the cross." After she told Tom what she knew, he leapt to the same conclusion she had: It had to be Jacques.

"I thought possibly Marie, especially when you said she knew about the Comte's still being alive," Tom said. "But the Comte tore that chain off his killer's neck. If she still has hers, then it must be Jacques' cross."

"Eliza doesn't think that Jacques could murder anyone. She was adamant," Jane said.

"And if he did," Tom mused, "why would he strike the Comte in the back two times with the first weapon and then again in the chest with a different weapon? It doesn't make sense."

Jane stared into the fireplace. "No, it doesn't," she agreed.

"I wish I had met this Comte, even once," Tom said. "Tell me about him."

"I didn't know him very well," Jane protested. "Eliza married him when I was a child. I saw him but rarely. I didn't even recognize him when he accosted my carriage that day."

"But you have met him several times in the past few days," Tom argued. "Describe him to me as if he were one of your characters."

Jane straightened up in her chair, captivated by the challenge. She closed her eyes. "He was handsome and had a fine figure. You saw the cleft in his chin. His eyes were most unusual—a tawny yellow. His manners were charming, just roguish enough to be interesting."

"I am jealous of a dead man," Tom murmured.

"His dress was striking. His scarlet scarf was a flamboyant splash of color."

"Did you say scarlet?"

She opened her eyes. "Yes. Why?"

Tom pointed out the window. "Like the one that man is wearing?"

An older man, wiry and leather-faced, was standing in the road, staring at the Austen house. He was dressed like a poor laborer except for the splash of scarlet around his neck.

"That's the Comte's scarf!" Jane cried. "That man must have been at the church!"

"He might be the killer," Tom said.

Without pausing, Jane jumped to her feet and raced outside.

CHAPTER 20

The truth rushed on her; and how she could have
spoken at all, how she could even have breathed,
was afterwards matter of wonder to herself.

MANSFIELD PARK

"Albert Jones!" Jane shouted after the fleeing man. "I know where you live, so you might as well stop!"

As if she had jerked hard on a tether, the man stopped. He stood in the middle of the road, knee-deep in snow, and waited for her to catch up. "Miss Austen," he said. "I didn't know it was you." He was dressed in a motley assortment of coats and vests and he hadn't shaved in several days. Even in the crisp winter air, Jane could smell the odor wafting from his clothes.

"You were staring at my house," Jane said severely. "Who did you think it was?"

Panting, Tom joined them. "Jane, are you a lunatic?"

"Mr. Lefroy, let me introduce you to Mr. Albert Jones; he works on my father's farm."

Tom gave Albert a quick nod. "How do you do?" Then, to Jane, "Don't ever do that again! How was I to know you knew him?"

"Albert, where did you get that scarf?" Jane asked.

His eyes darting from Jane to Tom and then to the ground, Albert muttered, "I found it."

"Where?" Tom asked. "And when?"

"Last night. I found it by the side of the lane."

"The lane that leads to the church?" Jane asked.

Nodding, he quickly unwrapped the scarf from his neck and tried to hand it to Jane. "I didn't know it was yours, Miss Austen. Here you go."

Ignoring his gesture, Jane asked with urgency, "Exactly when did you find it?"

"Just before dawn. The snow hadn't stopped yet."

"What were you doing outside at that hour?" Tom asked suspiciously.

"I was out for a walk?" Albert said hopefully.

"You were poaching again, weren't you?" Jane asked. He started to edge away as though he might bolt.

"Poaching is illegal," Tom said in a stern voice.

"Stop being a lawyer for a moment," Jane whispered. "You'll frighten him and he won't tell us anything." Raising her voice, she said, "Albert, it's all right. Poaching is the least of our concerns."

"I'm not surprised when you have unburied corpses in the graveyard," Albert said and immediately looked as if he regretted it.

"Albert, what did you see?" Jane asked kindly. "I promise you won't get into trouble."

Albert examined her face for a moment; then he nodded. "I was out last night setting my traps. When the snow stops, the animals get confused. Good trapping then." He paused. "The best rabbits are in the woods behind the church, so that's where I was going. But when I got to the churchyard, there was someone there. A big man, with dark hair, carrying a lantern." His voice trailed away.

"What was he doing?" Jane prompted, dreading the answer.

"He was killing a man," Albert said in a low voice. "Stabbing him right through the heart! I hid behind a tree because I didn't want to be next."

"A large man," Tom repeated.

"Did he stab the man in the front or the back?" Jane asked. She was rewarded with an admiring glance from Tom.

"He was kneeling in the snow and plunged a knife into his chest," Albert answered with relish.

"Then what did he do?" Jane asked.

"He looked around the clearing about the church. I tell you, I thought I was a dead man. But he wasn't looking for me. He went up to that old yew tree and put something in that little hiding place."

Jane knew exactly what Albert was talking about. She asked, "Did you see what he was hiding?"

"No." Albert held up his hands to ward off danger. "And I don't want to know!"

"What happened then?" Tom asked.

"He went into the church. A few minutes later he came back out. He was carrying a satchel."

"It was dark and snowy," Tom said. "How could you see?"

"I said he was carrying a lantern, didn't I?" Albert said sulkily. "Then he went back to the parsonage."

"How do you know he came here?" Jane asked. "Did you follow him?"

"Not likely." Albert snorted. "I waited until he was out of sight and then went home by the lane myself. His footprints turned in at the parsonage's gate." He hesitated and scratched the stubble on his chin. "He dropped that scarf in the lane. I suppose he didn't notice. I thought that since the chap was a murderer and a thief, I had just as much right to the scarf as he did."

Tom opened his mouth, no doubt to lecture Albert on the niceties of the law, but Jane forestalled him. "Albert, why did you come to the parsonage today?"

"It's my mother. I told her the story and she said I had to tell Reverend Austen what I knew." He grimaced. "She won't give me any peace until I do."

"Would you recognize the man if you saw him again?" Tom asked. "It was dark and snowy."

"I'd know him again," Albert retorted.

"Thank you, Albert," Jane said. "You've been most helpful. My father is away, but we'll take care of the situation. Now go home."

"And the magistrate will want to see you," Tom warned, "so don't go anywhere."

"Magistrate?" Albert yelped. "Telling Miss Austen was one thing, but I don't want anything to do with the law."

"I'm afraid you won't have a choice," Jane said with sympathy.

"Will I have to mention the reason I was out?"

"Yes," Tom said shortly.

"Not at all," Jane said at the same moment. Glaring at Tom, she said, "Albert, you can say you were out for a walk."

He tipped his cap and scurried away.

Jane started walking purposefully back to the house. "I need my coat, Tom. Then we can go."

"Go where?" he asked.

"To the yew tree. I daresay it will be the clue that solves this murder!"

"Wait for me, Jane," Tom complained, slipping in the snow. "Why do you walk so infernally fast?"

Jane smiled, but did not slacken her stride.

"Did he mean that enormous tree in front of the church?" Tom asked.

"That tree is where we hide the key to the church. It's such a long walk to the church, my father wanted to make sure that anyone with business there could get in."

"Who knows this secret?"

With a sidelong glance, Jane grimaced. "Most everyone in the parish."

"So a stranger like Jacques wouldn't know it was a common hiding place?"

"No," she confirmed.

"His bad luck," Tom said.

Jane's steps quickened. Her boots made no noise in the powdery snow. She could hear Tom breathing heavily behind her, trying to keep up. They reached the clearing and Jane pointed to the yew tree that towered over the church. Legend had it that the yew was seven centuries old, dating back to when the church was a medieval building, part house of worship, part fortress.

There was a large knothole in the trunk, just above Jane's head. Gingerly, she felt around in the hiding place with a gloved hand. She touched something metallic and cold. A round shape . . . no, it was long and narrow. She finally caught hold of it and drew out a pair of scissors. And not just any scissors: dressmaking scissors with long blades.

"What did you find?" Tom asked from behind her.

"Scissors," she said, holding them up to the winter sun. Dark streaks marred the blades.

"Is that . . ." he asked.

"Blood? Yes, I think it may be," she said. "I think we found the first weapon. Not two blows to the back, but one blow with two blades." She was thinking furiously. "I think I know who killed the Comte," she said. "But I don't know why."

"Who?" Tom asked, mystified. "How can a pair of scissors tell you anything?"

"I've seen these scissors before," Jane said. "They belong to Marie."

"But she had her necklace. You said that you believed she was innocent."

"So I did," Jane mused. Her thoughts were racing. Marie had a necklace. Was it the one she had worn before—or someone else's?

Eliza had said that her husband had given one to Marie's husband and to his brother Jacques. What if Jacques had replaced her lost one with his? Jacques was Marie's brother-in-law and uncle to her son. The boy. Marie's boy.

Suddenly the truth was blindingly clear to her. "I have to go back to the parsonage," she said. She shoved the scissors at Tom. "Take these. The magistrate will want them." She took off at a run.

"But, Jane! Who did it?" Tom called.

"I must go!" she shouted over her shoulder.

Jane had never traversed the distance between the church and her home so quickly. Tom had no chance of keeping up with her, and she was glad for other reasons that she had left him behind. Unraveling this tangled skein of facts and motivations was exciting, as enjoyable as getting a bit of prose exactly right, and Jane didn't want to share the moment with anyone.

At the parsonage, she rushed in past her mother.

"Jane, I think I have a rash!" Her mother's plaintive voice followed her up the stairs.

"Not now, Mother!" she called. Jane hurried to the sitting room she shared with her sister. Under her breath, she said, "Cassandra, I wish you were here right now." But perhaps Cassandra had left the next best thing. Her sketchbooks were on a low shelf.

Jane knelt on the floor and pulled out a handful of sketchbooks. After a moment, she found one from six years earlier and flipped through the pages. Familiar faces and scenes leapt off the paper, but not what she was looking for. She picked up an earlier sketchbook. "Ah," she breathed.

Cassandra's clever pen had captured a perfect likeness of Eliza holding her two-year-old son, Hastings. But it was the image of the boy that most interested her.

Unlike Eliza's miniature, Cassandra's likeness was an honest rendering. Jane pulled out Marie's locket. She had noticed before that it was expensive. But what servant had a miniature portrait of her little boy? Only the most privileged sort of person could afford that.

Jane compared Marie's son, Daniel, with Hastings. Hastings' eyes were not quite focused, but he and Daniel had the same tawny-colored eyes. Both boys had dimples in their chins that would one day expand to be clefts. It was unmistakable: Hastings and Daniel both resembled their father.

"What are you doing, Jane?" Eliza's voice made Jane start. "Is that one of Cassandra's sketchbooks?"

Jane scrambled to her feet. "I'm sorry, Eliza."

"For what?" Eliza asked, her voice becoming thin and high-pitched.

"Because you are going to have to find a new maid," Jane said, her eyes fixed on Eliza's face. "I think Marie killed Jean."

"That's preposterous!" Eliza sputtered in astonishment. "She was grateful to him. He asked me to keep her as my maid even when she was with child. She would do anything for him."

There was no easy way to tell Eliza, so Jane steeled herself to just say it. "Jean was the father of Marie's son."

Eliza staggered back. "But little Daniel is eight. That means Jean was with Marie . . . He asked me to hire her . . ." She couldn't finish the sentence.

"I'm sorry. But the resemblance is clear." Jane wondered that Eliza had never remarked upon it herself, but then Eliza rarely confronted uncomfortable truths.

Eliza sank into an armchair. "I wish I could say I don't believe it. But knowing what Jean did to save himself, I realize I didn't know him at all." She looked up at Jane with imploring eyes. "But why would Marie kill him?"

"I don't know," Jane said, sitting on a battered settee, "but he was not the man you thought he was. Perhaps he betrayed her, too."

"How do you know it was Marie?"

"She used her special dressmaking scissors to do it. He must have torn her necklace off her neck as he staggered to the ground."

"But she had her necklace!" Eliza was grasping at straws.

"I think Jacques has been protecting her. He replaced her necklace with his own. He left a knife in the corpse and hid the scissors. He hid Jean's things—perhaps in the barn. He's been in and out of there all week taking care of your horses."

Eliza stared at a spot where the brown wallpaper was peeling from the wall. "But why?"

A voice from the door startled them both. "Why? I'll tell you why." Marie's beautiful face was transformed from a servant into a Fury. She stepped inside the room and shut the door behind her.

Jane's breath quickened when she heard the turning of the key in the door. Marie turned to face them. She had a coat folded over her arm, hiding her right hand.

"Daniel was Jean's son," Marie cried. "He should have been the heir! He's healthy and will grow strong. Hastings never will." Eliza caught her breath, but Jane didn't take her gaze off the maid.

Marie went on, the resentments of almost a decade spilling out. "But I was content so long as Jean took care of us. He arranged for me to marry René, who was kind enough. He pretended Daniel was his son so we were safe, and indeed, he was a good father to my boy." Her voice trembled. "But Jean's thoughtlessness got René killed. And Jean left me in the dark even longer than you. When it was I who loved him."

She glared at Eliza. "You pretended to mourn, but you were quick enough to start dancing and entertaining. Not even a year, and you have your eye on that young Mr. Austen! But I suffered! I had lost the man I loved."

"He wasn't worthy of love from either of you," Jane argued.

Marie shrugged. "But I did love him. I would have done anything he asked. When I thought he was dead, my love died too. And then, c'était un miracle! Madame told me he was alive; I thought he had come back for Daniel and me. But I followed you that night. I crept into the church and heard everything." Tears streamed down Marie's cheeks. "He said he wanted to bring Madame to America. He was going to leave me here." She dashed away the tears with the back of her hand. "That I could not forgive. I waited until you two left, with your high-and-mighty words. Then I confronted him. And do you know what he said?"

Jane was silent, confident that Marie would tell her everything.

"He said that if I would steal Madame's jewels and money then I could go with him." She clenched her fists.

"First he made me a fool. Then he wanted to make me a thief. I told him I wouldn't do it. He was so angry with me that he stormed out of the church."

It was impossible that they could be in a house full of people but still fearful for their lives. But Jane knew Marie was capable of killing; they weren't safe locked in a room with her. Sick with fear, Jane still couldn't keep from asking, "Did you drop one of Madame's handkerchiefs then?"

"By mistake I dropped one that Madame had discarded. Madame thinks she is being kind when she gives me her fine things that she no longer wants. As if I should be grateful for her leavings."

"I thought we were friends," Eliza said weakly.

"We were never friends, Madame."

"But those times you took care of me when I was sick?" Eliza wailed. "How often did you comfort me when I despaired about Hastings' health? Are you saying that was all a lie?"

Marie, for the first time, looked uncertain. "Perhaps not. But did you ever comfort *me*?"

"I never knew how you suffered," Eliza said sadly.

Jane's eyes darted between the two women. Whether she had acted intentionally or not, Eliza had done well to remind Marie of their shared past. Jane and Eliza might still leave this room unscathed.

"He acted as if my feelings were of no account, either," Eliza said sympathetically. "He never understood either of us."

Marie shot Eliza a surprised and grateful look. In a low voice, she said, "I told him I would expose him and tell the world that he was alive and that he had let two men die for him."

"That would ruin him . . . and me," Eliza said.

Jane pictured the scene. The handsome count striding angrily out into the snowstorm. The wronged woman following him into the churchyard.

"He hit me." Marie's hand touched her cheek. Jane looked closely and could see a bruise there, partially hidden by cosmetics. "He told me that I was insane. He said that if I did what I threatened, he would take Daniel away with him to America. I would never see my son again."

"What did you do?" Jane asked, although she thought she knew.

"When he started to walk away, I pulled the scissors from my skirt." Jane nodded; she recalled the special pocket Marie wore around her waist for her dressmaking shears. "Then I stabbed him in the back."

Jane and Eliza were stunned by Marie's bald confession.

"He staggered and tried to keep his footing by holding onto me. But I was finished helping him! I shoved him away but he grabbed at my throat. He caught my necklace—the one he had given my husband—and tore it from my throat."

"What did you do then?" Jane asked in a hushed voice.

"I came home," Marie said simply. "I told Jacques every-thing. If I were to hang for murder, I wanted him to take care of Daniel. He convinced me that Jean was a man who deserved killing. He killed René. Jacques said it was an eye for an eye."

Marie dropped her coat. She leveled the Comte's pistol at Jane and Eliza. "Now to take care of you and Madame."

CHAPTER 21

*"I have heard it all; and how you will explain
away any part of your guilt in that dreadful
business I confess is beyond my comprehension."*
SENSE AND SENSIBILITY

*E*liza leapt to her feet and stood next to Jane. "Marie, don't shoot!" She grabbed her cousin's hand and clung to it tightly.

"You don't want to do this," Jane said urgently. "Marie, you're a mother—could you really deprive little Hastings of his own mother?"

Marie's eyes widened, and the hand holding the pistol wobbled.

"You killed the Comte, yes. But he was a despicable man who had treated you badly and abandoned you and your son," Jane went on, pouring all the persuasion she had into her words. "But it is a far cry from that to murdering us." Jane knew the power of words; murder was a particularly ugly one. Her body trembling, she waited for Marie's answer.

Marie dropped her hand to her side. Jane rushed forward and snatched the gun. She handed it to Eliza, a veteran of a hundred shooting outings and familiar with guns.

Breathless, Jane took Marie's arm and led her to the settee. "Marie, sit down. We'll do our best for you with the magistrate, I promise."

"I cannot hang. What will Daniel do without me?" Marie buried her face in her hands.

"Jane, look," Eliza said in a low voice. She held out the pistol. "It was not even loaded."

"Marie, what were you planning to do?" Jane asked.

Looking down, Marie said, "Jacques has arranged for me to leave. Immédiatement. Today while he was in Basingstoke, Jacques sent word to our friends to collect Daniel from Madame's house. Once we were together, I would have disappeared. I'd go somewhere far enough away that English law could not touch me."

"The French might even have welcomed you back with open arms," Jane observed.

"They wanted the Comte de Feuillide dead, and now he is." Marie straightened her back and lifted her chin. "I have letters from Jean that prove Daniel is his son. If there is ever a possibility of recovering the Comte's estate, Daniel will be waiting." She rummaged through her pocket. Jane tensed, but then relaxed when Marie pulled out a handkerchief. One of Eliza's, naturally. Marie dabbed at her eyes.

"Why did you come to my room, then?" Jane asked, puzzled. Surely, Marie's best option had been to run as quickly and as fast as she could. Marie's hand went to the base of her throat.

"You came back for the locket?"

"It is the only portrait I have of my son," she said simply. "It will be my solace in prison."

Without a word, Jane dropped it into Marie's hand.

"Merci, mademoiselle." Her tears flowed freely. Suddenly she was kneeling in front of Eliza, holding out her hands to her former mistress. "Madame, I know I have wronged you. But I only did so out of love. Please, let me go."

Over Marie's head Eliza and Jane exchanged a long stricken look. Jane shook her head. She wasn't going to let Eliza's sentiment interfere with punishing a murderer. Even one as pitiable as Marie.

"We are sorry for you, we truly are," Jane said. "But the authorities will be here soon."

"Miss Austen, do you want me to be hanged? I have no choice but to run. And then I'll be no use to Daniel at all."

"You'll never get away," Jane said.

"Please," Marie whispered.

"Jean has caused enough grief," Eliza said suddenly. "We cannot let him claim another life. Jane, how can we help her escape?"

Jane blinked, for once at a loss for words. "It's no small thing you are suggesting, cousin. We'd be breaking the law." She winced, thinking of Tom's reaction to what she was contemplating.

But was it so wrong? The Comte had been a despicable man. He had been the cause of the death of two men. Marie had been his victim as much as his murderer.

"Jane, our duty is to another woman. A mother!" Eliza said, tapping her slippered foot impatiently.

The law was clear—but was it right? Daniel would be an orphan unless Jane helped his mother. Her inaction would be responsible for ruining that little boy's life. For what? Justice for the Comte? A man who deserved none. Could she live with that? She rather thought she could not.

She sat at Eliza's dressing table, wishing for a pen and paper to help her plot an escape. "You have transportation?" she asked Marie.

"Jacques has arranged a horse. I can ride."

"That's not good enough. A young woman traveling alone is too conspicuous. And the horse will have to rest. You'll get to London faster in Eliza's carriage."

"Yes, take my carriage!" Eliza said eagerly.

Marie backed up half a step. "I cannot drive it!"

"Jacques can," Jane replied.

Marie's eyes went to the ceiling as if she were praying. "Jacques can say you forced him to drive you," Jane said, pointing at the pistol. Eliza handed the gun back to Marie.

A tapping at the door startled them. "Jane? Jane, are you there?" It was Tom's worried voice.

"Since when are you so well acquainted with Mr. Lefroy that he comes to your room?" Eliza whispered archly.

"Sssh," Jane hissed.

Tom raised his voice slightly. "Jane, open the door. Your maid said you were in your room. I must see you!"

With a finger to her lips, Jane instructed the others not to speak. She went to the door and opened it a crack.

"Yes?"

"Jane, you ran away like a hound on the scent . . ."

"Are you comparing me to a dog?" Jane asked with a small smile. Behind her, she heard Eliza stifling a laugh.

"Not at all, I didn't mean . . ." Tom sputtered. "I thought we were past playing games."

Jane took a deep breath. "So we are."

"When you ran away," he said, "I thought you had solved the puzzle. Do you know who killed the Comte?"

Jane glanced at Marie, her back pressed to the wall, clutching her locket in her hand.

Tom would not forgive what Jane was about to do. But she had already decided that Marie's need was greater than Tom's precious law. "I was wrong," she said finally.

His face fell. "That's too bad. Why don't we discuss the circumstances? Together I'm sure we can find the solution."

Jane hesitated. "It's not seemly for you to be outside my bedroom door. Wait for me in the parlor; I'll be right down."

Tom shook his head. "James and your mother are in the parlor. Don't make me wait in there."

Jane half-smiled. "My father's study, then. It's in the back of the house. If anyone asks, say you are looking for a book. That is the only excuse anyone would need in this house."

"Very well," Tom said reluctantly. "But hurry. We have much to talk about." Jane abruptly shut the door in his face.

"What shall we do?" Eliza asked.

"I sent him to Father's office because it is on the far side of the house from the stables. He won't see the carriage leave, I hope," Jane said. She gripped Eliza's hands. "Get whatever money you have. Then you and Marie must go to the stables. Jacques must be back soon. Have him harness the horses. The snow is melted enough that you can get through. When all this dies down, Jacques can bring her carriage back to Eliza."

Marie nodded mutely.

"And Mr. Lefroy?" Eliza asked.

"I'll distract him as long as I can." Jane dug in her pocket and pulled out the two gold chains with the identical crosses. She turned to Marie. "Take these. They belong to you and Jacques."

"Bless you, Miss Austen," Marie replied fervently.

Before Eliza slipped out the door, she said, "I know something about men—more than you, my dear cousin Jane—and if Mr. Lefroy realizes you've helped Marie to escape, he shan't forgive you."

"I know," Jane said bleakly. The choice had come upon her so quickly, but even if she had infinite time to decide she felt she would come to the same decision.

Jane stayed in her room for a few minutes, picking up a book, brushing her hair. Anything to use up some time. Finally, she could dawdle no longer.

She started downstairs. When she reached her father's study, she steeled herself before opening the door.

Tom was pacing in Reverend Austen's office. "Finally!" he said. "I don't understand you. Everything in our investigation was at breakneck pace. Until now. How can you slow down when we are so close to the end?"

"Even a bloodhound gets tired," Jane said, not meeting his eyes.

"Let us go over the ground again," he said. "I've taken the liberty of jotting down some notes. First . . . "

Jane cut him off, more sharply than she intended. "Tom, forget about the murder!"

He raised his eyebrows. "Are you all right?" He led her to the battered leather sofa. "Sit down. I knew you would feel the shock sooner or later."

Jane let herself be led. Tom thought she was a weak-minded woman who would swoon at the thought of a little murder. Well, it was as good a way to keep him occupied as any.

"Thank you," she said in a weak voice. "Perhaps you could pour me a glass of sherry?" With a languid hand she indicated the decanter. Tom hurried to pour them both a glass of the straw-colored liquid.

"You look pale," he said. He reached over and brushed a stray lock of hair from her forehead. "I think you had better rest. We can talk later."

She put her glass on the side table and caught his hand in her own. She pressed it against her cheek, wishing she could tell him the truth. But Marie's safety depended on Jane lying to Tom. He must not go looking for Marie or Jacques.

"Jane!" he cried in a low voice. He leaned in and kissed her lips. She was overwhelmed with the sense of him. His cologne, the sweet taste of sherry on his lips, his shoulder touching hers.

She closed her eyes, trying to commit every detail of the kiss to memory. Sitting there, Jane wished they would have many more intimate moments together. But even in the warmth of that moment, she knew it was fleeting.

Outside there was the unmistakable sound of a horse neighing and the sound of carriage wheels in the snow. Tom unceremoniously leapt to his feet, abandoning Jane on the sofa. "Your brother must have seen reason and brought back the magistrate." He headed for the door.

"Tom, wait," Jane called, but it was futile. He was rushing to the front door. She followed more slowly. When she caught him up, he was staring down the lane, puzzled. "That was your cousin's carriage. Is she going somewhere?"

"No," Jane answered.

"Then where is it going? The snow has melted a little, but it's still rough traveling."

Jane took a deep breath. Marie was safely away. There wasn't a horse or carriage in the village that could catch her. By the time Tom managed to do anything, Marie would be long gone.

"Jacques is taking Marie to London," she said.

"Marie? But we haven't talked to her yet. Those shears are very suspicious . . ." His voice trailed off. "Marie did it, didn't she?"

Jane nodded.

"And you knew. Did you know she was running away?" There was a note of pleading in his voice.

The temptation was there. Tom wanted her to lie to him; that was clear. If Jane could bring herself to dissemble, she and Tom might have a future. There might be other kisses and arguments and reconciliations. All she had to do was lie.

"I knew," Jane admitted. "I helped her."

Looking down the road, he murmured, "I should go after them."

"Marie has the Comte's pistol," Jane said quietly. No matter that the gun was not loaded; she just needed to dissuade Tom.

He stared at her for a long moment. "Do you realize what you've done?"

She nodded, her eyes fixed on his face.

"I cannot protect you when the magistrate finds out what happened."

Her eyes narrowed, she asked, "How will he know?"

As though it were self-evident, Tom said, "Because I will tell him."

"Even if I will be prosecuted?" Jane asked. She sighed inwardly; she should have seen this eventuality. Tom's principles were deeply held.

"Of course." His eyes were wounded, but as he spoke he became angrier. "Absolutely no one is above the law." He turned on his heel and went back inside.

Jane waited on the porch, rubbing her arms against the cold. It felt like a penance she should endure. A few minutes later Tom returned, wearing his greatcoat. Suddenly formal, he bowed. "I've said my farewells to your mother. I shall take my leave, Miss Austen."

Then he strode toward the stable and out of her sight.

CHAPTER 22

"He has broken no faith with me."
"But he told you that he loved you."
"Yes—no—never absolutely. It was every day
implied, but never professedly declared. Sometimes
I thought it had been, but it never was."
SENSE AND SENSIBILITY

*J*ane's head was pounding with the exquisite agony of an awl boring its way through her eyes. She had hardly slept the night before, between worrying about Marie, reliving her brief embrace with Tom, and wondering where Henry was. He had looked in briefly in the afternoon, after everyone had left, but then he had disappeared.

She had heard footsteps on the landing in the early hours of the morning. She had opened her door a crack to see an exhausted Henry, carrying his muddy boots. He had paused in front of Eliza's door, but thought better of knocking and continued to his own room.

The breakfast table was practically deserted. The toast sat uneaten on the sideboard. Henry and Eliza had not come downstairs. Eliza had sent a message by Prudence that she would miss breakfast but would join them for church. James was already on his way there. Jane's body went rigid with tension. Even James couldn't miss a corpse in his vestry.

"Did you quarrel with Mr. Lefroy, Jane?" Her mother's querulous voice seemed to add a rasp to the awl.

Steeling herself for the obligatory scolding, Jane said, "Why do you ask, Mother?"

"He left quite abruptly. And he wouldn't look at me when he took his leave. What happened? Things were going so well between you. I was thinking you'd made a match at last."

Rubbing her temples with her fingers, Jane answered, "We had an irreconcilable difference of opinion."

"You mean you couldn't be amenable," Mrs. Austen chided. "What harm would it do to let the gentleman win an argument occasionally? You will never marry if you can't climb down from your high horse. And if you don't marry, how will you live? Your father and I won't be around forever, you know!"

Jane let her mother blather on. Her eyes were fixed on the window, watching for James to come running down the lane with news of a body in the vestry. *At least when the Comte is found*, she thought, *Mother will have something more interesting to worry about.* And as the daughter of a reverend, Jane would be relieved to have the Comte properly buried in consecrated ground.

Henry appeared in the doorway. Mrs. Austen immediately shifted her complaints to his appearance. "You look like you haven't slept in a week, nor bathed! And your hands, Henry! Were you in a fight?" Without waiting for an answer, Mrs. Austen went to the sideboard and began assembling a plate for Henry.

Henry yawned and sat down next to Jane. She twisted her neck so she could see: His knuckles were bruised and cut and his nails were filthy.

"What were you doing last night?" she whispered.

"I'll tell you later," he promised. His eyes were bloodshot and he needed to shave.

"What about James?" she asked. "He's at the church now!"

"Little sister, have I ever let you down?"

"Frequently!"

Henry's face split in a wicked grin, and Jane relaxed. She didn't know what he had done, but his confidence reassured her.

"What are you two mumbling about?" Mrs. Austen asked.

"Nothing, Mother," Jane and Henry said in unison.

"The two of you will be the death of me," she complained. "Now finish your breakfast. James is expecting us to be punctual."

Henry muttered something under his breath about what James could do with his punctuality. Jane elbowed him in the side and he nearly spilled his tea.

Promptly at the hour of departure, Eliza came downstairs. She looked as lovely as always. Perhaps only Jane noticed how simple her toilette was without a lady's maid to help her. Henry's eyes lit up when he saw her, and Eliza's return smile was full of promises.

As Jane buttoned her pelisse, she thought how typical it was that Henry and Eliza, the most feckless players in this melodrama, would prosper most once the dust settled. And Jane? What would happen to her? A fairy-tale ending with Tom Lefroy? Not likely.

The Austens joined the line of villagers going to the church. The bright sun was warm to the skin, and the snow was melting apace. It made for a muddy lane, yet Jane couldn't help but think that the more the snow melted, the more evidence of wrongdoing would disappear, too.

Henry was walking arm in arm with Eliza ahead of her. Jane caught up to them. "Eliza, dear," Jane said, "I must borrow Henry for a moment."

Eliza's lighthearted demeanor froze. "Is everything all right?" she asked.

"I don't know," Jane said.

"Everything is fine," Henry assured them. "Eliza, I shall return in a moment."

Jane drew him to one side of the lane. "What did you do with the body?" she demanded.

"I acted like the soldier I am." He grinned. "I took direct action to solve the problem."

Eyebrows lifted impatiently, Jane waited for him to explain.

"Yesterday, I went into Basingstoke and spoke to . . . well, I cannot tell you his name. Suffice it to say that Edward told me who to go to if something untoward were to happen."

"I would say that murder qualifies," Jane said dryly.

"Particularly when the body in question belongs to a French aristocrat who is already presumed dead," Henry agreed. "They were very concerned that this matter be dealt with speedily. And discreetly."

"Does this discreet action involve the marks on your hands?"

He nodded. "Last night, the War Office sent two men to help me. We buried the Comte deep in the woods. It wasn't easy; the ground was frozen in spots."

"You didn't bury him in the churchyard?" Jane asked, aghast.

"Of course not," Henry retorted. "How could that be kept a secret?" Henry's direct gaze dared her to argue.

Reluctantly, Jane had to agree. "And that's the end of it?" she asked. "There'll be no investigation?"

"Of what?" He lifted his shoulders. "The death of a dead man? The Comte was killed a year ago by a rogue government. He left behind a beautiful widow and son. That is the end of the story."

Jane considered. It was the end. Even the clandestine burial had the approval of the English government. With no body, there was no crime. Marie and her son could safely leave the country without fear of reprisals. Eliza had escaped the taint of scandal. As had the Austens. It was over.

As they walked, the church came into view. Jane averted her eyes from the graveyard where she had found the Comte's body. The clearing was filled with scatterings of people. Their cheerful conversation seemed to be cleansing the space, making it fit for worship and joy again.

James was waiting at the doorway. When he saw them he came striding over. His black robes flapped behind him, reminding Jane of a massive crow. Given her recent experience with crows, the thought was an unwelcome one.

"Jane!" he said. "I'm very disappointed in you."

Jane's eyes darted to Henry, who lifted his shoulders. "Why?" she asked warily.

"The church is dusty. There are footprints everywhere! It was your task to clean it." His aggrieved tone made it clear that he took her neglect personally.

Letting out a breath she hadn't realized she was holding in, Jane was uncharacteristically apologetic. "I'm sorry, James. I neglected my duties."

"You were scribbling your little stories, no doubt!" he said scathingly. "Don't let it happen again."

Holding onto her temper with effort, Jane simply nodded.

In that instant, James was distracted by the sound of horses trotting in the lane. Jane followed his eyes to see Tom Lefroy on horseback. Mr. Bigg-Wither followed. From the glare he gave to Tom's back, it was obvious that the magistrate blamed Tom for forcing him outside on a winter morning.

They dismounted. Tom nodded briefly to James, but ignored the others. Jane heard her mother draw in an offended breath.

"Reverend Austen," Tom announced, "we are here about a murder."

Mr. Bigg-Wither pushed his way in front of Tom. "I am the magistrate for this parish. I'm here to investigate the crime. This young man simply reported it."

"A crime?" James asked. "At my church?"

"At Father's church," Henry muttered under his breath. "It's not yours yet."

"Yes," Mr. Bigg-Wither said. "I'll trouble you to let us examine the vestry."

"There's a body there," Tom said. "And Henry and Jane Austen know all about it."

"So nice to know who our friends are," Henry said to the sky.

Tom looked determined but miserable. Jane bit her lip, of two minds about Tom Lefroy. No one liked a talebearer, but Tom had only done what he thought was right.

"A body? That's absurd." James's face reflected his puzzlement.

"I must insist that you let us search the church," Mr. Bigg-Wither said.

"Very well," James conceded. "Please hurry. The bells are ringing for the start of my service."

Tom and Mr. Bigg-Wither jostled to be first through the narrow door, but Mr. Bigg-Wither's bulk won the day. James followed.

Left behind, Henry stood close to Eliza. She took his hand and held it tight, regardless of who might see.

Mrs. Austen turned to her daughter. "Do you know anything about this, Jane?"

Jane shrugged. The seconds ticked by like minutes, but soon enough Mr. Bigg-Wither stormed out of the church.

Tom was on his heels, remonstrating. "Sir, we must search. The body cannot be far."

"If there's a body at all!" Mr. Bigg-Wither retorted. "I'd heard you were a bit wild. Let this be a lesson to you about the perils of drinking too much."

"But I tell you—"

Mr. Bigg-Wither cut him off. "Your imagination has embarrassed my office, not to mention dragging me out in the snow when my lumbago is acting up. I'll thank you never to mention this again unless you want me to take it up with your distinguished uncle!"

Tom, furious, shut his mouth. Staring stonily at Mr. Bigg-Wither, he waited until the magistrate had ridden away. Then he turned to Jane. "Where is it? I know you are behind this."

"Me?" she asked, a hint of asperity in her voice. "I'm just a misguided woman; how could I dispose of a body?"

"Then your brother," he said, glaring at Henry. Henry started to step forward, but Eliza held him back. Jane appreciated her tact; Tom Lefroy was Jane's problem.

"Whatever was done was sanctioned," Jane warned him. "You will do yourself and your precious law career no favors by insisting otherwise."

Tom drew her farther from the others. His face was bleak. "Jane," he implored in an intimate voice that tugged at her heart. "You know this was wrong. You've circumvented the law and allowed a murderer to go free. This is beneath you."

Jane considered what he was saying carefully. In the cold light of day, did she still believe that it was more important to show Marie compassion than it was to hang her as a murderer?

Yes, she did. Even the entreating look in Tom's wide dark eyes couldn't convince her otherwise.

"We saved the lives of two people: Marie and her son," Jane said. "All you did was destroy any possibility of our future together. I shan't regret what I did. Shall you?"

Tom stared at her, and she gave herself the luxury of enjoying his handsome features, until she reached the accusation in his light green eyes.

She walked away from him into the church. A boy was in the bell tower, hanging on to the bell ropes. The pealing of the bells filled her ears but could not crowd out the sharp pang of loss.

"Goodbye, Tom," she said quietly but did not look back.

Dear Cassandra,

Now that my adventure has ended as abruptly as it began, at least I have the solace of writing to you again!

Madame Lefroy has just left the rectory. She tells me Mr. Lefroy has left the district, I suspect never to return. Or at least not return to me. So you may set your worries for my reputation aside. It's very amusing, is it not? Tom and I might have overcome the traditional impediments of poverty, distance, and nationality (did I tell you that he was Irish?) only to founder on philosophical differences. Well, perhaps it is not so amusing after all.

Earlier today, I put aside my pen to go for a walk. I needed to clear my head. I visited George. It was very soothing to have my conversation limited to what I can say with my hands.

We did have one awkward moment when George asked after Tom. He gets so few visitors and George had liked him so much. But a bag of Cook's special toffee sufficed to make him happy again.

I had ample time walking to and fro to come to terms with my circumstances. I knew the moment I lied to Tom about Marie that he wouldn't forgive me. I was right. He could not, or would not, I am not sure which, circumvent the law for what seemed to me to be an even nobler purpose.

I wish Tom well. I'm certain he has a grand future in front of him. Only to you will I admit that I wish it could have been with me.

Henry has proposed to Eliza, and needless to say she has accepted him. It's rather cruel of Henry to ask James to officiate at the ceremony, but then Henry always did have an uncomfortable sense of humor. With Eliza's connections and fortune to back him, we may expect his swift rise in the ranks.

Eliza is preparing to return to London and tell Hastings the news. Poor boy, he is inconsolable without his friend Daniel as a playmate. And you will not be surprised to hear that Eliza is inconsolable without a maid to help her pack. She takes some comfort that her coachman has returned. We have not had any news of Marie, so we assume she made it to France safely.

This letter grows long and costly, but there are still things I want to tell you that should not be put on paper, even now. Come home, Cassandra, and I will recompense you for the luxuries of Godmersham with a new story.

Imagine a gentleman with five daughters and no fortune. The business of his wife is to get her daughters married. The two eldest sisters might resemble us: one who is sweet and kind like you, and another who is too clever for her own good. Of course there will be dances, misunderstandings, heartbreak, and at least one engagement. No murder, however. I am done with that.

With best love,

Jane

*J*ane Austen was born in 1775, the second youngest of seven children. Her sister Cassandra, the elder by almost three years, was the only other girl in the family and Jane's close confidante. Cassandra called Jane "the sun of my life." They usually shared a room and when they were parted, would write almost daily letters.

Cassandra's letters from Jane are our primary source of information about Jane's personal life. They are funny and full of biting commentary about their friends and acquaintances. Jane felt comfortable enough to say what she really thought to Cassandra. Unfortunately, Cassandra destroyed most of the letters after Jane's death (one historian estimates that only 160 letters remain out of a possible 3,000). It was the custom to destroy casual correspondence in the 19th century, but Cassandra may also have respected Jane's wishes that her private thoughts remain private.

The Austen siblings did not have much money. Their father, a country reverend, had a limited income. After launching his sons' careers, there was little left to provide dowries for his daughters. In 1794 Cassandra was engaged to a poor clergyman named Thomas Fowle. They could not afford to marry right away and settled on a long engagement. Unfortunately, he died of fever in the West Indies three years after he proposed.

Jane's relationship with Tom Lefroy is one of the great near-romances in literary biography. Jon Spence's biography, *Becoming Jane Austen* (later adapted as the movie *Becoming Jane*), claimed that Jane had a serious relationship with young Mr. Lefroy. In fact, we only know that he visited his uncle in nearby Ashe, during which time he danced several times with Jane. She wrote about him to Cassandra, saying he was a "gentlemanlike, good-looking, pleasant young man." She also called him her "Irish friend" and downplayed their relationship by telling her sister, "I do not care sixpence" for Mr. Lefroy.

But Cassandra must have heard rumors and clearly cautioned Jane about her reputation. By return letter, Jane confessed that she and Tom had been doing "everything most profligate and shocking in the way of dancing and sitting down together."

But Tom left in January of 1796, never to see Jane again. He would settle in Ireland, marry an heiress, and have seven children. His career would prosper, too; by 1852 he would hold the exalted post of Lord Chief Justice of Ireland. As an old man, he admitted to his nephew that he had been in love with Jane Austen, by this time a famous novelist, but he called it a "boyish love." Perhaps it is only a coincidence that he named his first daughter Jane.

Jane did not lack for marriage proposals. The best-documented one was in 1802. Jane was a spinster of 27, an age at which women were considered unmarriageable. Much to her surprise, an old acquaintance, the young Harris Bigg-Wither (whom we met at the Assembly Ball), proposed. Harris, although the heir to a large estate, was socially awkward and stammered. However, he felt comfortable with Jane, a lady he had known for many years. She accepted.

The benefits to Jane were obvious. She would be lady of a fine house and be able to help her parents and forward her brothers' careers. Cassandra would always have a home. Jane herself might become a mother. But within hours, she realized she had made a terrible mistake. Perhaps, as some biographers suggest, she remembered the joy and giddiness of her flirtation with Tom Lefroy. In any event, she called off the engagement early the next morning and fled the scene ignominiously. The Bigg-Withers were furious and the Austens dismayed. Harris married another woman and had a large family. Despite the social pressures on Jane to wed, she would never marry.

Jane had four brothers. James, the oldest, was a clergyman and eventually succeeded his father as the reverend at Steventon. After his first short-lived marriage, he eventually married another woman with a difficult temperament for whom Jane did not care at all. Francis and Charles were in the navy and rose to the rank of admiral and rear admiral respectively.

Jane's brother George lived until his seventies. He was rarely talked about in the family, although he was a particular favorite of Jane's. The biographical record is unclear about George's illness; possibly today he would be diagnosed with cerebral palsy. It is believed that he was unable to speak or hear, because Jane knew sign language and wrote of "talking with her fingers." At this time there was no official sign language, but many individual ways to communicate with the deaf. Small wonder that Jane warms to Tom Lefroy when she discovers he can "speak" with George in *Secrets in the Snow*. There is some evidence that Tom had a deaf sister.

The only son Reverend Austen didn't need to support was easygoing Edward, because he had been adopted by the Knights. Wealthy cousins of the Austens, the Knights needed an heir, and their solution suited the penniless Austens well. Jane and Cassandra were frequent guests at his grand estate, Godmersham.

After Mr. Austen's death, Mrs. Austen as well as Jane and Cassandra were left in a precarious financial position. Edward gave them a cottage in Chawton, where they lived out the rest of their lives. This cottage is now the Jane Austen Museum.

Jane and Cassandra lived a quiet life, but they were well informed about world events, especially the war with France. They had two brothers hoping to make their fortunes in the navy, and for a time, Henry was in the army. Unusually for the time, their father encouraged them to read widely and